His father shivered involuntarily and said, 'I never thought it would come to this.'

'We're ready for it,' Max replied.

The old man sighed. 'Is anyone ever ready for this? It will be a holocaust.'

'It won't last long, Father. Six months, maybe a year. The English and French won't really fight. They'll put up a show and then they'll do a deal. That's what the Führer forecasts.'

'My God! Let's pray that he's right.'

Patrick Kelly is the pseudonym of a writer well known in another field.

Patrick Kelly

Codeword Cromwell

A MAYFLOWER BOOK

GRANADA
London Toronto Sydney New York

Published in paperback by Granada Publishing Limited in 1981

ISBN 0 583 130062

First published in Great Britain by
Granada Publishing 1980
Copyright © Granada Publishing 1980

Granada Publishing Limited
Frogmore, St Albans, Herts AL2 2NF
and
36 Golden Square, London W1R 4AH
866 United Nations Plaza, New York, NY 10017, USA
117 York Street, Sydney, NSW 2000, Australia
100 Skyway Avenue, Rexdale, Ontario, M9W 3A6, Canada
61 Beach Road, Auckland, New Zealand

Set, printed and bound in Great Britain by
Cox & Wyman Ltd, Reading
Set in Intertype Times

Granada ®
Granada Publishing ®

This one is for Heinz and Geneste

One

Old Fenwick was enjoying himself on the rostrum . . . it was the fortnightly market auction where everybody knew everybody else. When it came to Lot 74 he did his best to make the two gas brooders, the chick feeders, and the drinking fountains, sound like the Crown Jewels. There were only two bidders, Major Mason (Retd) and Charlie Cook from Winchelsea. And Charlie was only bidding out of bloody-mindedness because Mason wouldn't rent him the thirty-acre field for wintering some of his ewes. Lot 74 was finally knocked down to the major at £11.50 and afterwards Charlie helped him slide the wooden box into the station wagon to show that there was no ill-feeling.

Rye is an awkward little town to get out of during the summer when the visitors take over, so Mason kept to the bottom road and was back at the farm in just over twenty minutes.

It was the two Calor-gas canopy-brooders he had been after. Not for day-old chicks but for newborn lambs in February. The old wooden box smelt of creosote, and as he lifted out the canopies he laid them carefully on the grass. The feeders and drinkers were in good condition although the galvanizing was a bit rough in places. There was a nice old copper maximum and minimum thermometer for hanging on a wall, a few spare parts for the brooder valves, and a piece of faded yellow oilskin cloth with a couple of elastic bands around it.

It was nearly an hour later, when Mason was sitting on

the bench under the tree having a cup of tea, that he remembered, and walked across to the car and brought back the waterproof package. The rubber bands disintegrated as he slid them off, and the yellow waterproof crackled as he folded it open. It stank of mildew and wet basements. There were two books inside and half a dozen papers. They were damp, and stuck together in a solid soggy mass. The top book was about half an inch thick with a pale green paper cover. The title on the cover was *Die Sonderfahndungsliste Grossbritannien.* At the bottom it said *'Nur für Offiziergebrauch: Kriegsministerium Berlin'.* The second was thicker and only the edges of the pages were damp. The title was *Handbuch für die deutsche Besatzungsbehörde in Grossbritannien.*

There was an SS identity card in the name of Sturmbannführer Maximilian von Bayer, born 6 January 1912. The identifying photograph had been torn off and as Mason held the damp card in his hand it fell slowly apart into two separate pieces.

He turned back to the first book and peeled open the pages. It was green with mildew, and the paper swollen with dampness. His German wasn't all that good, but as he read he realized that it was some kind of Black List of people in Britain whom the Germans were going to arrest after their invasion. They were mainly names that Mason had never heard of. There were hundreds of names, and a lot of official abbreviations in German that he couldn't understand. The names were numbered and he looked carefully down the left-hand page of the open manual. They were an odd mixture of names.

90. Cooper, Ivor, Mitgl. d. brit. Rüstungsausschusses, London, The Old School House, Rudgewick (Sussex), RSHA iii D2.

91. Copeland, Fred, RSHA VI GI.

92. Coralfleet, Pierre, richtig: Frank Davison, vermutl. England, RSHA IVE4.

93. Cormack, Georges, Direktor, zuletzt Riga, vermutl. England, RSHA IV E4.

94. Coudenhove-Calerghi, Richard, 17.8.94 Tokyo, Schriftsteller, vermutl. England (Osterr.) (Legitimist), RSHA IV A8.
95. Courboin, brit. Agent, zuletzt Brüssel, vermutl. England, RSHA IV E4.
96. Coward, Noël, vermutl. London, RSHA VI GI.
97. McCracken C, 18.7.80 London, brit Oberleutn., zuletzt Brüssel, vermutl. England, RSHA IV E4.

The second manual contained the orders for the German occupying forces from the Reichsführer der SS Heinrich Himmler. Folded in two, and tucked inside the book, was an order from von Brauchitsch, the German army's Commander-in-Chief. It was dated 9 September 1940 and stated that after the occupation 'all able-bodied British males between the ages of seventeen and forty-five would be dispatched immediately as slave-workers in Europe'. The instructions were chilling even though it was all long past. Executions, hostages, confiscation of food and houses and terrorization of the civilian population were to be the order of the day. It was to be a deliberate policy of plunder and revenge.

He pulled apart the last slab of damp papers. Some of them were quite illegible but there was a letter in English, faded and blotched but still readable. The handwriting was youthful and round, a feminine scrawl with flamboyant crossings of *t*'s and dottings of *i*'s. It was still in its original envelope post-marked Cambridge and addressed to 'Max von Bayer, Schloss Eger, Hildesheim, Niedersachsen, Deutschland'. The letter was written in brown ink and there was a purple German censorship stamp on both sides of the single sheet.

Dear Max,

How are things with you?

Things look very bad at the moment, and over here we wonder what will happen. Daddy said that he had heard that you were at your Embassy in London last year, why didn't you come up to see us??? Will you have to serve in the army when you have so many other responsibilities?

David (the swot) got a double first and is hoping to do a post-graduate thing on German guilds in the fifteenth century. How ridiculous! Who cares?

I'm in my second year now at the Guildhall, but what happens at the exams in December I can't bear to think.

We all send our love and if you are over here please, please, please come and see us.

Yours affec.

Sadie.

There was an address in Cambridge and a telephone number. It was dated 1 September 1939.

There was a British identity card in the name of Barnes, M., and a ration card with only the butter ration used.

Out of mild curiosity he checked the dialling code for Cambridge and dialled the number. The operator cut in almost immediately. Cambridge didn't have six-figure numbers any more.

He put the stuff in the bottom drawer of his old desk and forgot about it.

Two

The girl lay back on the slope of the river bank, her eyes closed against the sun. Her dark hair fanned out on each side of her face, her white, even teeth biting on a long stalk of grass as the young man looked down at her. Her skin was pale despite the freckles on her neat, pert nose, but her mouth was poppy red, full and tempting.

The young man's hair was almost white and it lifted softly in the breeze off the river. He was reading silently from an open book that was resting on the girl's stomach. He shifted one supporting arm as he held the pages open.

'Can I read you a verse, Sadie?'

'OK.'

The young man cleared his throat and with only the faintest of accents began to read out loud.

'O if thy pride did not our joys control,
    What world of loving wonders should'st thou see,
    For if I saw thee once transformed in me,
    Then in thy bosom I would pour my soul.'

The girl turned her face to look at him, her brown eyes protected from the sun by his shadow.

'Who is it, Max? Shakespeare?'

'Sir William Alexander, Earl of Stirling.'

The girl closed her eyes.

'Go on then. Finish it.'

'Then all thy thoughts should in my visage shine,
    And if that aught mischanced thou should'st not moan,

Nor bear the burden of thy griefs alone;
No, I would have my share in what were thine.
And whilst we thus should make our sorrows one,
This happy harmony would make them none.'

They were silent for a few moments and then the girl struggled to lean up on one elbow, shading her eyes with one hand as she looked across the river.

There was an echo of laughter from a girl in one of the punts, and faintly they could hear a portable gramophone, a man's voice and a piano; they could just hear the words carried on the breeze – '. . . You were there . . . I saw you and my heart stopped beating . . . you . . .' and then there was the sound of the St John's bells ringing out across the river and the park, drowning all other sounds in a welter of joyful crashing metal.

The young man reached out and covered her hand with his.

'Will you be coming to the gymkhana tomorrow?'

The girl sat up and pulled at a tuft of grass that had been missed by the mower. She looked up at his face.

'We're all going. The Howards are coming too.'

'I wish it were just you, Sadie.'

The big brown eyes were still on his face and her head was tilted slightly, in a reassuring and slightly submissive gesture.

'There will be other days, Max.'

The young man sighed as he looked back at her.

'Do you like me, Sadie?'

'Of course I like you, Max. We all like you.'

'I'll win you the red rosette tomorrow. You see.'

She laughed softly. 'Don't break your neck or we shall get hell from your father.'

He looked up quickly. 'Why don't you like my father?'

'We do. He's just a bit . . .' She shrugged.

'Arrogant?'

'Well, maybe not arrogant. But he *is* a bit bossy, isn't he?'

'He *is* a Baron, after all.'

She looked at him, smiling. 'Of course, of course, it isn't

that. He's just a bit overpowering, he needs smoothing down, that's all. His feathers are always a bit ruffled.'

The young man half-smiled. 'Mother used to do that, but after she died he had nothing except his business to keep him going.'

He looked at his watch. 'It's time we were on our way, it's nearly seven.'

He stood up, brushing the grass cuttings from his trousers, and then he held out his hand and pulled so that the girl was standing. Hand in hand they walked along the river bank towards the footpath at Trinity Bridge.

Sadie Aarons was nearly seventeen, and in a few months' time was due to start her first year at the Guildhall School of Music. Her father's influence had been used to circumvent the age limit, but the shortage of budding 'cellists, especially pretty ones, had also helped.

Moshe Aarons was Professor of German at King's, and his son David was one of his students; his wife Rachel was a doctor at one of the local hospitals. They were a close-knit family, relaxed and easy-going. Moshe Aarons was only the second generation to be in England, and under the amiable exterior was an animal awareness that would have surprised most of their friends. An awareness of the realities of life that came from being the son of a Jewish refugee from Kraków, who had arrived in England with £50, a violin, and a degree in music from Warsaw University. A degree that had allowed him to earn a meagre living for his family, playing daily in a quintet at a Bournemouth hotel. When Lev Aarons obliged with yet another encore of 'Pale hands I loved beside the Shalimar' he played as if his life depended on it. And in some ways it did. He had been more at home when World War I and a collapsed lung had made it possible for him to sit behind a desk with the Hallé in Manchester. When Moshe Aarons watched his father from a gallery seat at the Free Trade Hall he learned more than he realized about dedication and determination. From Manchester Grammar School Moshe had won a place at King's, and from then onwards Cambridge and the college had been his home.

Rachel Stein had been one of the first Jewish girls at Newnham. They had married when they were both twenty-two. Grandfather Aarons had died just over a year ago on 26 April 1937. The day the Germans bombed Guernica in the Spanish Civil War.

Maximilian von Bayer was twenty-six, handsome, a graduate of Göttingen University and the only child of Baron von Bayer, whose vast estates between Hanover and Brunswick had withstood the nightmare of hyper-inflation and provided funds for certain industries that the Herr Baron had seen as vital to Germany's survival. Ludwig von Bayer asked nothing in return, beyond a low rate of interest and a generous attitude towards his business and personal tax assessments. He was not uninterested in German politics; indeed there were some who said that it was his views passed on to Brüning that spelt the beginning of the end of the Weimar Republic. He had joined no political party, and gave no overt support to any politician. But there were few week-ends when there were not half a dozen statesmen and leading politicians accommodated at his sprawling mansion set on the slope of the hills.

Max von Bayer had had an English tutor from his eighth birthday. The Herr Baron was an admirer of the English. An admirer from a distance. He had never been to England and had no language other than German. But the Englishmen he had met in the course of business had had a special kind of arrogance that he found admirable. They knew what they wanted, were indifferent to continental subtleties and custom, and took it for granted that what they wanted they would get. They were only mildly impressed by his palatial home and its treasures. His business interests ranged through property, steel foundries, chemicals, textiles and banking. He had a mistress in Berlin, a city which he visited frequently, and another, a young girl in the village, who visited him only at his hunting lodge in the woods. He was not a happy man, but he was a contented man, because he gave no time to analysing and philosophizing. He was a man of action.

His son Max was something of a disappointment to him.

8

He was tough and healthy, but there were strong elements in the young man's character that were too much like his mother. He never criticized his father, but there were times when those blue eyes looked at him with doubt, as if they knew something about him that he didn't know himself. A silent sitting in judgement, an unwillingness to join his father's world. These things were excusable in a pretty woman but dangerous in a man. Too much Schubert and not enough Wagner. Too much dreaming and not enough doing.

There were, however, mitigating circumstances. Young Max von Bayer was a horseman. He rode for the German Olympic team and a special showcase had had to be built to house all those silver cups and engraved salvers that he brought back, smiling, from every country in Europe. And he was a good boy. He gave no trouble, and that was more than you could say for some rich men's sons who spent their time whoring in Berlin or chasing ballet dancers.

Max von Bayer had taken his degree in German history at Göttingen, and had been given, as a present, a year at King's to improve his already almost perfect English. And it was there he had met Sadie Aarons. She had been just fifteen but in one of her mother's flowered hats and a lime-green organdie dress she had looked several years older. He was thankful that she had an older brother which made it possible for the three of them to spend most of their free time together. He had been made welcome by the family although he was conscious of their amiable amusement at their daughter's suitor. Because a suitor he was, from the very first day.

In the summer of the second year they had been invited as a family to the von Bayer's, and the young man's loyalties had been torn in two. There was, as his old professor at Göttingen would have put it, no meeting of minds. Despite Professor Aaron's perfect German, the two older men might just as well have been trying to converse in Mandarin. The academic trying to show an interest in the machinations of big business, and the businessman desperately trying to hide his boredom about Grimm's Law or some variety of medieval German.

The young man had watched with an eagle eye for any indication that his father was being patronized or despised. But there was none. He loved his father almost for the first time in his life for his efforts to entertain his friends, who in turn were charming about every treasure displayed for their approval. But his love was for the effort, and his loyalty was for the girl with the dark brown eyes and the long slender fingers. All concerned were relieved when the week was over and they could get back to their normal lives. Max had stayed for another week with his father before hurrying back to Cambridge.

Kind, well-contrived words had been said by both sides about the other, but the experiment had not been repeated. A counter-invitation had been issued to the Herr Baron, but unfortunately prior business commitments had made it quite impossible for him to accept.

After two weeks of feeling like a traitor to his father, Max von Bayer had settled back in the warm bath of the family Aarons.

Sadie Aarons had tried hard to be interested in gymkhanas and point-to-points, but the genes for such things had not been passed on even from those Polish forebears. But for two whole summers she had criss-crossed East Anglia with horse-boxes and curry-combs, watching the young man with the fair hair persuade a chestnut gelding named Attila to take water-jumps and double-oxers in its stride, to prove how much he loved her. He was naturally competitive but not thrusting, and the English liked him a lot. But when he had got it into his head that winning was synonymous with love, then nothing but a first was good enough. For an international-class rider, the local gymkhanas were not all that difficult, but he walked courses and practised as if every event was the Olympics.

She watched him as he sat well-down in the saddle on the chestnut. Shading his eyes against the late afternoon sun, waiting alongside the Irishman to see if there would be three for the jump-off or just the two of them. As always, his hand came up from time to time to touch the peak of his riding hat. It was a reflex, a habit, a bringer of good luck. He told her that Len Hutton did it too. He did it again, and she smiled as he did it a third time, because at the third time he always searched for her face in the crowd, and he was looking at her now. She waved and he took off his hat to her. If he had been an Englishman it would have been a half-joking gesture. But for Max von Bayer it was a knight to his lady. His thick blond hair was too much for the black velvet riding hat. It covered his ears and the back of his neck. The fair hair should have made him look an archetypal German, but his strong handsome features had touches of almost feminine beauty. The eyes were heavily lidded like the eyes on a sculpture, and his mouth was sensuous with soft full lips, well-shaped and only just avoiding dimples at their corners. He was almost too handsome, she thought, but the saving grace was that he seemed totally unaware of his attraction. She had seen adult women, as well as young girls, overwhelmed by that radiant smile as he responded amiably to some banality.

Eventually there were only two for the jump-off and after the poles had been raised and a brick put back on the model wall, she watched him walk his horse round the new course. Unhurried, professional, missing nothing. Then he was back at the start and the loud-speaker boomed over the field. 'And the first to go in the jump-off is Attila, ridden by young Max von Bayer of Germany.' There was a spatter of clapping and then the bell. His hat had gone at the big gate and the chestnut had seen it from the corner of his eye and gone over diagonally, only just clearing the top bar. It was a timed round but von Bayer collected the horse expertly and headed for the water jump as if he had all the time in the world. They took the triple easily and there was a roar of relief when at the final wall a hoof moved a brick without dislodging it.

He ambled the horse through the crowd to her, wiping the sweat from his face with a big white handkerchief. He slid down from the saddle to stand beside her and touch her hand as they watched. The big black Irish horse had been overstretched at the first fence in the triple and went into the pea-sticks on the third with his chest, and with four faults the time no longer mattered.

Max rode into the ring for the cup and rosette and touched his cap to the MP's wife presenting the awards, and stood aside at the exit gate to allow the two runners-up to leave first. A girl shouted to him and he nodded and smiled, and touched his whip to his hat. Then he was riding over to where she stood.

There were two young Englishmen standing talking and laughing with her. Apart from the surge of jealousy, he resented the way these sorts of people took her for granted. Sliding their arms casually round her waist, and with no reserve in the jokes they told her. But she turned immediately to smile at him and he was placated. He left the chestnut with the groom from the stables. Ten minutes later they were both crowded into the front seat of the stable car, alongside the driver. He dropped them both at the corner of Silver Street and King's Parade and they took the footpath down to King's Bridge.

There was barely a ripple on the surface of the river, but a small and fitful breeze moved the tall heads of mace and yellow iris that grew at the edge of the bank. A mallard and her ducklings lay in a soft hollow on the slope of the bank, the orange light of the setting sun painting the small flat beaks as, with their heads turned, they rested on the soft down of their backs.

Max leaned with his elbows on the bridge, facing the girl. He took the crumpled red rosette from his pocket and held it out to her. As her hand reached for it he caught it and held it in both of his.

'Only another twenty days before I have to go back, Sadie.'

'I know,' she sighed. 'What does your father want you to do?'

He shrugged. 'Lawyer, banker, anything serious.'

'And what do you want to do?'

His blue eyes looked at her face. 'Just to be with you.'

She shivered slightly as the breeze freshened, sweeping the black hair across her face. She held out her hand for him to take.

'They'll be waiting for us, Max.'

Back at the Aarons' house there had been the standard congratulations on his win, and then they settled down to the cold salmon and salad, and strawberries and cream. They ate at the white table on the lawn in front of the french windows. There was so much laughter that only Moshe Aarons heard the telephone ringing. He walked slowly into the cool of the house.

He came back a few minutes later.

'Max, it's your father on the telephone.'

It was ten minutes before Max came back to the group in the garden. His face was drawn and white.

'I have to return home immediately, Mr Aarons.'

'Is your father ill, Max?' Moshe Aarons' eyes scanned the young man's face.

'No. Maybe it would be better if it were that. He has been told that tomorrow the German Army will be mobilized because of the Czechs.'

There was almost complete silence around the table and Moshe Aarons tried to ignore the stricken look on his daughter's face. He thought that maybe he ought to have warned her, because he had seen it coming when the Nazis had marched into Vienna in the spring. It was Rachel Aarons who broke the silence.

'Sadie, why don't you and Max stroll down to the Parade for a coffee. I'll pack Max's things, and your father will check the trains for tomorrow morning.'

'Right, Mamma.'

They sat in the dim light of the cinema café, the only occupants, and they could hear the faint, booming sounds from inside the cinema. They were showing 'Lost Horizon'.

'What do you think will happen, Max?'

'God knows. It depends on what the Czechs do.'

'What do you think they'll do?'

He shrugged. 'They'll do whatever London and Paris tell them to do. Goering was at our place the week end before last. My father says that Adolf Hitler is bent on war.'

'Will you be called up?'

'I'm not a reservist. I was excused because of my riding commitments.'

'So why do you have to go back?'

He looked at her troubled face, and said softly. 'Do you care that I go back?'

'Of course I do. We all do.'

'Why?'

'We don't want you to be in the fighting.'

'Nothing more than that?'

She saw the anguish on his face. 'We care about you, Max. I care about you.'

'I love you, Sadie.'

She blushed. 'I know you do, Max. It's nice.'

'But *you* don't love *me?*'

She smiled. 'I don't know, Max. I'm not sure I even know what love is. I like to be with you.' She shrugged. 'I just like you in every way.'

He put his hand across the table to cover hers, and immediately her hand turned upwards to hold his hand.

'I want you to marry me, Sadie. Before all this starts. Can I speak to your father tonight?'

'He'll say I'm too young, Max. And maybe I am.'

'Let me speak to him.'

'All right. We'll both speak to him.'

'No. It's the man's job to do that.'

She laughed softly. 'I don't see why.'

'It is, my love. Leave it to me.'

'We'd better go back or they'll all be in bed.'

Moshe Aarons had an inkling of what the subject of conversation was going to be and he took the young man's arm and led him into his study. He waved him to one of the brown leather armchairs and turned to his small drinks cupboard.

When he was sitting comfortably himself, and the two glasses of port were poured out, he spent a few moments lighting his pipe.

'So, Max. What did you want to talk about?'

'I want to ask your permission to marry Sadie.'

With raised eyebrows Aarons applied the side of his box of matches to the bowl of his pipe.

'You want to ask my permission to marry Sadie, or you want to ask Sadie to marry you. Which is it?'

'Your permission to ask her, sir.'

Aarons shrugged as he fiddled with his pipe without looking up.

'You don't need my permission to ask Sadie, Max. It's a free country.'

'I mean, ask her with your approval, sir.'

'She's only just seventeen, Max, and a very young seventeen at that.'

'I'm only twenty-six, sir. There would only be nine years difference.'

Aarons smiled. 'I know, my boy. I know. It's not only the difference in age, it's just that she's far too young. She isn't capable of real love as yet. She has had no experience of other young men. She's very fond of you. We all are. But she's a child.'

'Does that mean you have no objections, sir, apart from Sadie's age?'

Aarons looked up, and von Bayer wasn't sure whether his eyes were hard, or half-closed against the evening sun through the window.

'I'm afraid not, Max. I would see many problems for you both. They may not seem problems to young people in love, but problems they would be.'

'Can you enlighten me, sir?'

Aarons looked him in the eye. 'There's no point in dodging the issue, Max. We are Jews. Sadie is a Jew. In your country she would be open to persecution.'

'Not as my wife, sir. My father could guarantee that.'

'Nobody could guarantee that, and I would be a fool to let my daughter take such risks.'

'As my wife there would be no risks.'

Aarons spoke softly. 'In this country there are no such risks for her, married or unmarried.'

'So the fact that Sadie is Jewish is the major reason in your mind, sir?'

Aarons hesitated. 'No. I don't think you're right, Max. The problem is that *you* are a German. And your countrymen have laws that encourage the persecution of all Jews.'

'If all this blows over can I speak to you sometime in the future about this?'

Aarons leaned forward and touched his knee. 'Of course you can, my boy. Of course you can. You'd better get all your stuff together for tomorrow. We can always send on what you can't take, so don't burden yourself with inessentials.'

And that had been that. He shed hot, bitter tears in his room that night, and lay lonely and depressed until sleep had come with the first light of dawn. It was 12 August 1938 and Adolf Hitler ordered the mobilization of the German Armed Forces later that same day.

Three

He stood with the family, his legs straddling his two leather cases. His cups and prizes were packed carefully in Professor Aarons' old hat box.

As he was leaning from the carriage door he saw the tears in Rachel Aarons' big brown eyes and as the train pulled out slowly she said in a whisper, 'Don't let it happen, Max. Don't let them do it.'

The train stopped at Bishop's Stortford and Epping but he was not aware of it. His mind could see the study again. The old leather chairs, the shelves of books, the brass bowl with the overblown roses, the open window and the smell of newly mown grass. And Moshe Aarons with his pipe. The pipe that he filled or emptied to divert attention from what he was saying. Now, in the train, he was full of *esprit d'escalier*, but he knew that yesterday evening he had been clumsy and inept. Aarons had said nothing offensive, not even anything provocative. Just a logical facing of the facts. But he had been firmly put in his place.

The car was waiting for him at Ostend the next morning, and by the time they got to Düsseldorf he was asleep. At Bielefeld they were held up by tanks and armoured vehicles moving in convoy towards the Dutch frontier. Even on the autobahn to Hanover there were long lines of troop transporters with army motor-cyclists dashing like sheepdogs up and down the long convoys.

They turned off the autobahn for the Hildesheim road and his father was waiting for him at Schloss Eger.

They dined together that night and talked only of his riding and the cross-Channel journey back.

As his father picked at a bunch of black grapes he looked across at his son.

'What is it, Max?'

'I suppose it was a shock, Father, the mobilization.'

His father sighed without looking up from the grapes.

'You don't give a damn about the mobilization, my boy. What is it?'

'I had a disappointment, Father.'

'The girl?'

'Yes.'

'But you knew all along she was a Jewess. You knew that was the problem.'

'That wasn't the problem.'

'Oh. What was the problem?'

'That I am a German.'

'The father and the Nuremburg Race Laws, yes?'

'I'm afraid so.'

Ludwig von Bayer leaned back in his chair until it creaked.

'Did you sleep with her?'

'No, Father."

Von Bayer was too shrewd a man to say what he thought. That way he would only fan the flames and make the girl a martyr. He was glad that the affair had come to nothing, but he burned with hidden anger at his son being humiliated by a Jew. He had nothing against Jews. He did business with them, they kept their bargains, but they had always been separate. Coming out from their ghettos to try and outwit the people who allowed them their living-space. But their time had almost come. Others would square the account for his son. Meantime he would sympathize and say nothing to alienate the young man.

'Have you ever slept with a girl, Max?'

'No, Father.'

'There's a little girl in Alfeld. Very pretty. I'll arrange for you to meet her. It's time you had some experience.'

Although Moshe Aarons was no musician he was easily moved by music, and as he sat in his study he found it impossible to ignore the music that came from above, from his daughter's room. Again and again she played the same record. The first movement of the Elgar 'cello concerto. The lovely rhapsodic music that so well matched the fading sun on the summer garden obviously matched equally well his daughter's melancholy. She had made no protest, had asked no questions, but had played the Elgar and a setting of the old Jewish hymn of lament called 'Kol Nidre.' Again and again. There was nothing he could do, but he knew it was a signal of distress.

His son David heard the music too, and not being a father found no need to look for the perfect solution. He walked slowly upstairs and knocked on his sister's door. When there was no reply he walked in. She was sitting in a chair by the window looking out at the garden. She turned to look at him as the needle clicked monotonously in the scroll of the silent gramophone record.

'There's a yellow-hammer in the hedge, David.'

'And a bluebird watching it. D'you want to talk?'

'About what?'

'About Max.'

'There's nothing to talk about. He was sent packing and that's it.'

'He wasn't sent packing. His father wanted him home.'

'He wanted to marry me. He spoke to Daddy.'

'And what did he say?'

'Who knows? Neither of them told me. He must have said "No".'

'Did you want to marry him?'

She looked away, back across the garden.

'I don't know.'

'Isn't that a good enough reason?'

'Nobody asked *me*.'

19

The young man sat down on the bed.

'Do you know what the Nuremburg Laws are, Sadie?'

'No.'

'According to the Nazis, Jews are the source of all corruption, and are to be totally excluded from German life. It is prohibited for a German to marry or sleep with a Jew. Jews have no rights, no pensions, no protection. They can be beaten up by any Nazi thug, without even a pretence of reason, and have no recourse to the law.'

'This is just rumour, David.'

'It's not. They are laws. Hitler brought them in in 1935. Nazi officials take money openly to let Jews cross the frontiers.'

She turned to look at him.

'You're talking about Nazis, David. Max isn't a Nazi.'

'D'you remember when we went to the Kraski's place a couple of weeks ago?'

'Of course.'

'D'you remember that old man sitting on the chair in the garden?'

'The one who was ill?'

'That's the one. What illness do you think he had?'

'I don't know. Some kind of paralysis, I suppose.'

'That *old* man is forty-five. Younger than Father. He's Professor Kraski's brother. He was a judge in Hamburg nine months ago. They took away his job. He had no fortune and the Prof. and his wife got him out. It cost them five hundred pounds. He hasn't got any disease. Nazi hooligans beat him up in the street. Twice. That's why he can't keep still. That's why he's jerking and trembling all the time. He didn't do anything. He was a respected judge. All of that happened *just* because he's a Jew. For no other reason. Do you really think Father would let you go to a country where that could happen to you?'

'But Max isn't a Nazi. And his father is an important man. They wouldn't let anything happen to me. Anyway I'd be a German if I was married to Max.'

'You wouldn't, my love. You'd be a German Jewess.'

She sighed deeply. 'Do *you* like Max, David?'

'Heavens, yes! He's a great chap. I like him a lot. But I like Rabbi Mayer and I'd hate you to be married to him.'

She managed a dim smile. 'It's not really a joke, you know.'

At once his face was serious and he reached for her hand.

'Try not to be sad. It could all change in time. I'm sure he loves you. Just both of you wait, and it might all turn out right in the end.'

And she was mollified because 'both' was a linking word. It linked her to Max von Bayer as if it *were* all going to come right.

The following week-end von Ribbentrop and his entourage were staying at Schloss Eger. He wasn't a hunting man like Goering, and they all sat around talking after dinner on the Saturday evening. And von Ribbentrop prophesied that the Czechs would have thrown in their hands by the end of the month. The English and the French had no heart for a war. When he smilingly asked Max von Bayer his views on the English he listened carefully, and the young man was flattered.

Two days later there was a telephone call for him from Berlin. He was required to go that day to Berchtesgaden and assist with the translation of documents.

For the first time in two weeks the days passed quickly as he witnessed the negotiating teams, Chamberlain's and the Führer's, playing their games of spurious diplomacy. He served coffee to the principals, and heard Chamberlain talking volubly, not of the Czechs but of his fishing experiences in Scotland.

Two weeks later he was called on for the conference at Bad Godesberg, and the following day at Munich. And slowly, as he translated and interpreted for the second-line officials, he grew to despise the English negotiators in their eagerness to dispose of the Czechs. The grey-haired old man with his sallow complexion, the wet lips and the old-fashioned stiff collar was a Prime Minister. The head of the British Government. All he wanted was a piece of paper to take back to London and he didn't care what it cost, or who paid, so long as he stayed Prime Minister. Even his own junior officials seemed to despise him, and hid their humiliation behind schoolboy jokes. And the Frenchman Daladier made no pretence. If the Germans wanted Czechoslovakia they could have it, provided they took it discreetly.

A week later the German Army occupied the Sudetenland, and that looked like the end of the story. Not a shot was fired, and Hitler had had the guts to face them all, the professional statesmen of Britain and France; and with nothing but courage and conviction he had given Germany back her pride and her lost lands.

There were rewards all round, and Max von Bayer was sent to the embassy in London. He was attached to the embassy's commercial counsellor, but he was to report to von Ribbentrop direct. And once a week he wrote, by hand, his assessment of British morale and the gossip of the diplomatic parties.

In the first few weeks at the embassy he reached for the telephone a dozen times a day to call the number in Cambridge. It was almost unbearable to be in the same country as Sadie Aarons and not see her. But a mixture of pride and resentment prevented him from making the contact. There was one week-end when he drove half-way to Cambridge and then stopped the car. It wouldn't be the same. Her parents would be watching him, seeing him as a German, not just a young man. And on reflection, Aarons *had* been antagonistic. He had turned him down because he was a German. A Jew putting down a German. They cried out to the world that they were persecuted by the Germans and he had given a Jew the chance to strike back. He had been a fool. But he still loved the girl. She had been disappointed, he was sure, but they had had no opportunity to talk. Moshe Aarons had seen to that. They had had to say good-bye at the railway station as if they were strangers, with the family looking on, pretending they weren't all aware of the conversation in the study the night before. He blushed as he relived the humiliation. Maybe when the old scores had been settled with England and France he could come back and claim her. They would be glad to know him then, and *he* would be telling Moshe Aarons what the new facts of life were. He sighed, switched on the engine and turned the car for its journey back to London. Whatever his feelings for the girl, he mustn't give them a second chance to humiliate him.

He was at Schloss Eger during the second week in November when the pogroms against the Jews had started, and in Brunswick he saw the smashed shop windows after *Kristallnacht*, and the posters that prohibited Germans from patronizing Jewish shops. And for the first time in his life he experienced *schadenfreude* – a subtle, covert pleasure in others' misfortune. They had asked for it, and now they had got it. And they proved the Führer's point. All over the world their compatriots found the money and the influence to help them escape. They had no home-land, and they didn't need one, they owned the world. It was *their* tribal laws that made them different and separate, not the German Race Laws. Why blame the Germans for doing exactly what they practised themselves?

His reports to von Ribbentrop were never acknowledged but when he was home again for Christmas he was summoned to the Foreign Office, and a senior official questioned him about public reaction in Britain to recent events in Europe. When he was asked if he thought the British would go to war if the German Army occupied all of Czechoslovakia, he thought a long time before he replied. He said that he felt that they might declare war but that they would do very little. The public were against war and Mr Chamberlain had acknowledged that in his broadcast in September when he had said, 'How horrible, fantastic, incredible it is, that we should be digging trenches here because of a quarrel in a faraway country between people of whom we know nothing.'

The official made notes of von Bayer's comments and he was asked to wait. He waited around for four hours in the Wilhelmstrasse offices, and finally he was led into von Ribbentrop's office. The Foreign Minister looked up from the papers he was signing and pointed to a chair without speaking as he went back to his signing.

A few minutes later von Ribbentrop threw down his pen and pushed the pile of papers to one side.

'Well my boy, and how's that father of yours?'

'In good spirits, Minister.'

'Good.'

Von Ribbentrop stared at the young man's face before he spoke as if he were looking for some sign, some indication.

'It's been suggested that I'm wasting your talent having you in London. What do you say to that?'

'I'm sure it's not true, sir.'

Von Ribbentrop smiled wryly. 'There were those who said the same about me when I was there as Ambassador in '36. But in my case it was not meant as a compliment.'

Von Bayer made no comment and the Minister fiddled with a gilt letter opener that had Italian *fasces* for its handle.

'Have you done your military service yet, Max?'

'No sir, I was temporarily exempted because of my riding.'

'And now you are a diplomat and not liable, of course.'

The shrewd eyes watched von Bayer's face but there was no reaction, and von Ribbentrop leaned forward, his arms on the desk.

'I think we *are* wasting your talents, Max. There are more important things for you to do. Have you any objection to doing your basic three months' military training?'

'No, Minister.'

'In the SS.'

Von Ribbentrop saw the young man's look of dismay, and when his mouth opened he held up his hand.

'I know what you're going to say but I have my reasons. Your father is not a member of the Party. Neither are you. Nevertheless your father is much respected for his help and support. The Führer himself is well aware of his services. The work I want you to do will be invaluable if there is a war against England. But the same talents that I value would be snapped up by the Wehrmacht or the Navy and I don't want that to happen. With a commissioned rank in the SS you would be free of that problem. And apart from that I want you to learn how the Armed Forces work. Do you understand?'

'I think so, Minister.'

'You will go to Vienna for your training and then report

back to me. You'll get your instructions in a couple of days' time. I want you to do well on your course, understand?'

'Yes, Minister.'

Von Ribbentrop stood up. 'There's a party tonight at the British embassy. I'll take you along with my people.'

Four days later von Bayer reported to the SS barracks in Vienna, and settled into his new life like a hand into a glove. It was as if all his life he had been waiting to be a soldier. His enthusiasm and concentration delighted the instructors. They recognized a natural soldier and leader of men, and tested his ability and determination unreasonably. Von Bayer's group far outstripped all the others because von Bayer was a fanatic. Unorthodox but successful. Arrogant but not vain. And the only negative thing that they discussed at the final ratings conference they decided not to mention or record on his file. Von Bayer was a leader, but an undisciplined leader. He ignored orders that got in his way or might hinder his squad from winning. If he had been destined for the Wehrmacht they would probably have noted the failing, but he was going back to Berlin and the SS. And in Berlin he was not even to be on regular duties but permanently on detachment to the Foreign Office.

On the day he reported back to Berlin, Madrid surrendered to Franco's forces and the Spanish Civil War was over. It was 28 March 1939.

Von Ribbentrop was not available when he reported back to the Wilhelmstrasse, and he was given his briefing by an Abwehr colonel.

He was to go back to the London embassy but would operate independently. As a member of the commercial section he would gather all the information possible on military installations in southern England, with an emphasis on the south coast and the RAF. He would also report regularly on the morale of the general public and their attitude to Germany.

It was a hot day at the beginning of August when he drove up to Cambridge. He hadn't planned the trip. But the compulsion was overwhelming, and no sooner did the thought come into his mind than he was on his way. A feeling of guilt fought with the anticipation of seeing her, and he drove without stopping to the outskirts of the city. It was only when he was parking the MG that he realized for the first time that she might not even be in Cambridge.

He had walked to the end of the road and looked down towards the house. The upstairs windows were open, the curtains moving slowly in the light summer breeze. And on the opposite side of the road there was a barrage-balloon, swinging on its short cable, its silver belly rippling from the wind.

A postman had delivered mail, and a baker's van had delivered bread, but he had seen nobody leave the house. By the end of the afternoon he was tired and hungry and depressed, suddenly aware of the futility of his journey. Another half hour and he would go back to the car park. And with his eyes wide open he prayed that, if there was a God, Sadie Aarons would come out from her house. He had waited another hour before he walked back to his car.

He was driving unhappily down Trumpington Street when he saw her, walking with a young man, a music case in her hand. She was looking straight ahead, smiling at something he said, wearing a white dress covered with red roses, and a wide, black, shiny belt encircling her narrow waist. He pulled in to the side of the road and as he watched the young man slid his arm round her waist, and without hesitating she took his arm away, and, laughing, gave him the music case to carry. And with that gesture Max von Bayer had his reward. She looked just like he'd remembered her, a little taller, a little more self-confident, but the same youthful beauty, not yet a woman, still a girl. And she hadn't let him keep his arm round her waist. If the war clouds blew over, then to hell with his pride, he would come back to stake his claim, no matter what it cost.

He was recalled from London on 25 August and on the previous day he had sat in the Strangers' Gallery in the House of Commons and heard the debate that approved the

Emergency Powers Bill. The papers said that it was the hottest August day for thirty years.

On 3 September he was at home, and he sat in the study with his father, the radio tuned to the BBC. The chimes of Big Ben sounded particularly solemn, and then, sentence by slow sentence, he translated Chamberlain's declaration of war on Germany.

'I am speaking to you from No. 10 Downing Street. This morning the British Ambassador in Berlin handed the German Government a final note, stating that, unless the British Government heard from them by 11 o'clock that they were prepared at once to withdraw their troops from Poland, a state of war would exist between us. I have to tell you now that no such undertaking has been received, and that consequently this country is at war with Germany . . .'

His father shivered involuntarily and said, 'I never thought it would come to this.'

'We're ready for it.'

The old man sighed. 'Is anyone ever ready for this? It will be a holocaust.'

'It won't last long, Father. Six months, maybe a year. The English and French won't really fight. They'll put up a show and then they'll do a deal. That's what the Führer forecasts.'

'My God! Let's pray that he's right.'

Four

The Junkers-52 was wallowing and bouncing unpleasantly in the thermals from the hills below. One of the stretcher cases groaned as a kit-bag rolled against his leg, and a man who was strapped to a field-stretcher called for water, but nobody came. The doctors and nurses had stayed behind to administer the drugs and supplies that the plane had brought with them.

An SS officer with the insignia of a Sturmbannführer sat alongside the windows on the left side of the plane. His right leg was stretched out, braced against an ammunition box to keep his balance and the other was bent across the metal seat to support a talc-covered map fastened to a clip-board with a spring on each side.

It was his presence that had made the journey worse than it need have been. They were flying dangerously near stalling speed so that he could look over the terrain below. They were over von Kluge's 4th Army now, and he could see the roads crowded with broken-down vehicles and refugees, and smoke billowing from battered buildings. Just ahead of the plane he could see fires still burning in Béthune, and away to the north there was a pall of black smoke over Poperinge. Von Kleist's Panzer Group was smashing through to cut off the British who seemed to be heading for Dunkirk.

The grey-uniformed man got up and walked slowly and unsteadily towards the pilot's seat as the plane swung and shook in the evening air. He put his mouth close to the pilot's ear and a few moments later the plane shuddered and picked up speed as it headed for the airfield outside Aachen. He wondered why he was being dragged back behind the lines, and he wondered why the signal had ordered him to carry out this passing reconnaissance of the retreating British Army.

It was obvious that by the next night the British would be cut off from the sea and that would be the beginning of the end. They had been stupid to declare war when the invasion of Poland was virtually completed. And now the Belgians had surrendered, and the Dutch, and the Danes. The French were crumbling at every point where the Panzers touched them. With Allies like the French, decadent and demoralized, the British must have regretted their declaration of war even as they were making it. But now the Führer could deal with the British magnanimously; gallant losers respected by the victors. When Hitler had covered his Channel flank he would probably allow the British to have token units in the inevitable attack on Moscow. Winston had said harder things about the Soviets in his time than even Hitler himself had said. What a combination the two could make. Who would come out on top in the end? He closed his eyes in a moment of ecstasy. It was going to be fantastic. A new Europe. A new world. And in a moment's weakness he imagined himself in his uniform, mounted on the big grey; ahead of his troops as they marched down Silver Street in Cambridge. They would sweep left at King's Parade, she would see him, and then . . . he shook his head to dismiss the ridiculous thought.

The plane was banking steeply, turning to land into the wind. He held the leather strap alongside the window as the plane bounced heavily along the landing strip.

There was a staff car waiting for him alongside the wooden shack and he settled back into the comfortable rear seat of the big Merc.

The typewritten orders were from the OKW Forward Headquarters, and required him to report at the earliest possible moment to the Gauleitung at Cologne. All the traffic on the road was going the other way to join the armies thrusting into France. The journey would take at least two hours and he stretched out his legs and slid off his cavalry boots as he closed his eyes and settled back under the field-grey blanket.

It was four o'clock in the morning when they got to the Rhine bridge, and the pale pink fingers of the false dawn were already reflected in the heavy waters of the Rhine. As the car eased to a halt at the Gauleitung an army sergeant saluted and escorted him inside the building to the main foyer. At a desk with several telephones a colonel wearing a Knight's Cross with Oak-leaves looked the SS officer over as he went on talking on one of the telephones. When he replaced the receiver he said, 'Are you for Lion?'

The SS officer looked confused. 'I don't understand, sir.'

'Why are you here?'

'There was a signal, sir. I was ordered to report to the Gauleitung as soon as possible.'

'Your identity card?'

The SS officer unbuttoned his tunic and slid his hand inside. He brought out his SS identity card and handed it to the army officer who compared it with a list of names typed on two foolscap sheets. He ticked a name on the second page and handed back the ID card. He snapped his fingers and nodded towards an army lieutenant who walked across towards them.

'Take Sturmbannführer von Bayer to Room 459.'

'Yes, sir.'

It was another hour before he was escorted into the conference room and there were about thirty men already assembled there, sitting at the two long rows of tables. They were all officers and from all three services, most of them full colonels or their own service equivalents.

The seat he was shown to was not at the tables but in the corner of the room. The Wehrmacht colonel who had escorted him to the room bent down to whisper to him. He was to listen, say nothing, and when the meeting finished he was to report back to Room 459.

Then three men came in and the assembly stood to attention until the man in the centre of the cross table nodded for them to be seated. Von Bayer had seen pictures of the man.

He was General Hans von Greiffenberg, Chief of Operations of the German High Command.

His speech was brief. He announced that the Führer had instructed Admiral Raeder to start planning for the invasion of Great Britain. In the folders provided for them was background material which might be helpful, but it had been prepared back in November 1939. The operation was to be code-named 'Lion', a name chosen personally by the Führer. The officers present were to consider themselves as withdrawn from their regular units to become the planning staff for 'Operation Lion'. They would start work that day, 25 May, 1940.

There was no opportunity for questions, but the room buzzed with comment after the three senior officers had left. Von Bayer left and went straight to Room 459.

There was a man already in Room 459, sitting perched on the edge of the old-fashioned desk. his complexion was dark enough for him to be Italian or from the deep Tyrol, and his thin patrician face could well have been Roman. He nodded to von Bayer and held out his hand.

'Kästner, Otto. Abwehr, Berlin.'

'Von Bayer.'

'Yes, I know. Sit down.' He pointed to the worn leather chair. He sat himself behind the desk, his arms folded and resting on the leather top. His alert brown eyes scanned von Bayer's face before he spoke.

'You, too, are seconded to Operation Lion from the Foreign Office. And from now onwards you don't wear a uniform. You'll be working for me.'

He waited for von Bayer to respond and when he sat silently he carried on.

'You and I will have special responsibilities, working alongside the Operation Lion staff. You will at no time discuss our duties with anybody. And I mean *anybody*: generals, admirals and politicians included. If you are asked what you are doing you will describe yourself as a translator in the archive department. You will be given one of the special "Lion" identity cards that will allow you to go

31

anywhere, see any written material, and attend any meetings. Any questions?'

'What shall I actually be doing, sir?'

Kästner's brown eyes watched the young man's face, and, ignoring the question he said, 'You didn't choose to go in the SS did you?'

'No, sir.'

'What would you have chosen if you had had the chance?'

'A cavalry regiment in the Wehrmacht.'

Kästner half-smiled. 'Trotting up and down the Unter den Linden escorting the Führer I suppose.'

'Maybe.'

Kästner's eyes were suddenly like eagle's eyes, angry and predatory. 'Don't ever again be impertinent to me, von Bayer. In case you are not aware of it my rank is full colonel, and I stand no nonsense. Not even from rich men's sons.'

He sniffed, as if that established some proletarian quality. 'I arranged for you to fly over the English positions in France. What did you see?'

'They were making for the coast at Dunkirk. Our Fourth Army was heading to cut them off.'

'Will the English get away?'

'Not if the Luftwaffe give our people air-cover.'

'And the French. What will they do?'

'They are finished. I'd say that it's just a matter of weeks.'

'How many weeks?'

'Six or seven.'

'And what will the English do?'

'I don't know, sir. It would depend on the Führer's policy towards England.'

'What do you think that will be?'

'I had thought he might negotiate with their leaders but I think now that he may not.'

'Why do you think that?'

'We would not be here for Operation Lion if the Führer intended to negotiate.'

'Do you think the invasion will succeed?'

'I have no doubt, sir. It will succeed.'

'Tell me why you think that.'

'The British Army has been completely routed in this campaign. We can cut off their supplies by blockade. In air power we are superior, and in land forces too; there are only thirty kilometres of sea in the Channel for us to cross. Their morale is low. It must be.'

Kästner nodded. 'You and I will go to Bruges tomorrow with the rest of the staff. Where's your kit?'

'In Berlin, sir.'

'Listen. You take a couple of days' leave at home. I'll contact you there when I've found us suitable quarters.'

Except for short periods Otto Kästner had lived all his life in Berlin. He was born in the house in Dahlem where his mother still lived. His father had been a career officer in a cavalry regiment until he was released from a British POW camp in 1919, his lungs half-destroyed by the phosgene gas that had been blown back on the German lines by a perverse change of wind. His father had died when he was eight years old.

He remembered his father, not as the coughing invalid, but as a man who was handsome and charming. A man who never complained, but who lived with style on his modest pension and a small private income. They had seemed such a pair, his father and mother, like Dresden statuettes or something from *Der Rosenkavalier*.

When they had musical evenings his father would steal up to the small boy's room, put his dressing-gown on him and carry him downstairs to sit in one of the corners in a big armchair with some sweets or a piece of fruit. A tutor came for four hours each day, an old man who had once taught at the local *Gymnasium*.

The day his father died had been the end of the boy's good days. The house became silent, and his mother, tearful and rather petulant, was erratic now in her affection. Sometimes hugging him to her, and at other times totally indifferent to his presence. At first old friends had still called, but gradually they faded away as his mother's moods became an embarrassment. He had been almost ten when he woke up one evening, and heard his mother in the hallway. He wasn't sure if she was laughing or crying and he crept out of his room to look down from the banisters. She was with a tall man, vaguely like his father, his arms were round her and he was kissing her. He was wearing a uniform, the same kind of uniform his father had worn with those small rounded spurs at the heels of his boots. Without thinking he had cried out and the pair had separated, looking up at him. And the handsome man had said, 'A Peeping Tom for a son, I see.' He hadn't known then what it meant but he had been packed off to bed.

Major Kurrer had been a frequent visitor for several years, seeming to be more at home in the house than the boy himself, suggesting boarding schools that would turn the ninny into a 'real' boy. Young Otto Kästner recognized the influence that Kurrer had on his mother. He ignored the jibes and kept out of the way as much as he could. He still felt the same affection for his mother, for, young as he was, he knew by instinct that her new life was only a desperate attempt to blot out the happy past.

There were other male visitors who brought flowers and chocolates for the pretty widow. They generally hung around for a week or two and then disappeared. One who seemed to survive was a civilian, quite young, about thirty, an amiable man who appeared to like the boy. He was a cheerful man, casually dressed, and the boy's mother seemed to find him amusing.

There had been a party one November evening in 1933 when Otto was eighteen. The guests had been mainly service officers, and late in the evening Otto had found himself sitting at the top of the stairs with the amusing young man. He had brought Otto a glass of champagne and sat down beside him, watching the people below.

'What are they celebrating, Putzi?'

'The election results. A ninety-two per cent vote for the Führer.'

'I thought the Wehrmacht weren't keen on the Führer.'

Putzi laughed. 'They aren't, but they like the idea of an expanding Army.'

'Because it means promotion?'

'Yes. But these bastards won't make it.'

'Why not?'

'They're like prehistoric monsters. They think it's back to the good old days when they and their kind decided history.'

'I want to be an officer when I'm old enough.'

'Why?'

'My father was a career officer until he was gassed.'

'Of course. I forgot.' He looked at the boy. 'If they give you any trouble you let me know.'

The young man smiled. 'Thanks, Putzi.'

It was in 1935 that Otto Kästner went before the selection board. He needed all five officers' approval before he could be selected for a commission. Major Kurrer, now Lieutenant-Colonel Kurrer, was a member of the board. Otto Kästner had not been selected. It was his mother who phoned Putzi and told him what had happened.

Otto Kästner had been interviewed a week later by an official at the Foreign Office. It seemed that Putzi was a minor but influential member of the Führer's personal entourage. His commission had been countersigned by Joachim von Ribbentrop himself. He did his training at the SS cadet school at Bad Tölz. He was posted as an Obersturmführer to the planning staff at the Abwehr, as liaison officer. They barely hid their resentment at having to share their secrets with a junior SS officer, and Otto Kästner in turn despised their élitist old-world attitudes. Despite his junior rank his Party influence made him unassailable. They tried to get him off their backs, but they failed. He was a Nazi watch-dog on the military intelligence services, and he could stick his nose in wherever he fancied. And he did just that. Twice they had put in official complaints and twice he had been promoted. They learned their lessons slowly. He loathed the lot of them.

He was riding across the contour of the hill towards the big house, ducking under the wide spread branches of the chestnut trees, and the big grey was twitching her ears at the shadows from the leaves. Far away he could hear a plane, but otherwise everywhere was still and peaceful. He pulled

35

up the mare and stayed in the shadow of one of the old trees. There were wood-pigeons calling in the woods, and the herd of a hundred or so Friesians was lowing its way across the bottom meadow towards the milking parlour.

He wondered if she ever thought of him. He wondered too if Moshe Aarons was beginning to be afraid. All that singing about 'Hanging out the washing on the Siegfried line' must sound rather ridiculous now. They had got their army back from Dunkirk, and the BBC was doing its best to make it sound more like a victory than utter defeat. But England was lying there in the summer sun, like a ripe plum waiting to be picked. He wanted to be there when it happened.

His legs squeezed the mare's ribs and she moved off, picking her way carefully over tree roots and the hard dry ground.

At the stables the boy came out from the tack-room and took the horse's head. 'The Herr Baron said to tell you there's a gentleman waiting for you in the small conservatory.'

'Who is he?'

'I don't know, sir.'

'That martingale is too short, Hans. She can't recover quickly enough when she jumps.'

'Right, sir.'

He ducked as he went through the low door to the kitchens, and walked on through the sitting-room to the music-room to where double doors gave on to the small conservatory.

Kästner was sitting there alone in one of the wicker chairs.

'Sorry to break into your leave, von Bayer, but I thought it was better to talk to you here.'

'Would you like a drink? Try some of our own white wine. It's not at all bad.'

'No thanks. Maybe later.'

Von Bayer slid off his riding boots and wiggled his toes. To hell with Abwehr colonels. He was in his own home now. He turned to look at Kästner.

'Shall we talk then?'

'Tell me why you joined the SS, Max, not the Wehrmacht.'

'I was told to join the SS.'

'By whom?'

'One of the Party leaders.'

'Which one?'

'Von Ribbentrop.'

'Are you a member of the Party?'

'No.'

'Is your father?'

'No.'

'Why not?'

Von Bayer shrugged. 'I'm not interested in politics.'

'Are you interested in winning the war?'

'Forgive me, Colonel, but what is all this?'

'I'll explain later. What do you think about the Wehrmacht?'

'I never think about them one way or another. They do their job, we do ours.'

'It was the SS who set the pace through the Low Countries and France. Their casualties were higher in proportion than the Wehrmacht's.'

'Is that official?'

'It's fact, my friend. And it will be the same when we go East.'

'What are you trying to tell me?'

'You and I are going to look and listen to everything that is planned for "Lion". If it had been left to the generals we shouldn't have occupied the Rhineland, or Austria or Czechoslovakia. We shouldn't have conquered the Poles and we shouldn't be planning "Operation Lion". They were against them all. The Führer gave them the orders, they just did what they were told. There are people who don't trust them to do what they're told. You and I are to watch them, and report on what they are up to.'

'Why us, Colonel?'

'Because certain people trust us. We both know England well, we both speak fluent English, and we both have reputations for criticizing anything that gets in the way of victory.' He smiled coldly. 'I've seen your training report and talked to the instructors. They reckoned that you were being wasted on routine duties. And my colleagues see me as too unorthodox for the Abwehr. We should get on well together.'

'Who do we report to?'

Kästner smiled. 'You report to me.'

'But it was Admiral Raeder who suggested "Operation Lion" to the Führer.'

'True. But people can get cold feet. You and I are there to keep a look-out.'

'Spies on our own people?'

'Observers.'

Kästner stood up. 'I've taken us a place at Quai de la Rosaire 57. Take another day's leave and then report to me there.'

Five

Kästner and von Bayer sat engrossed, each at his desk, as they read the Führer's Directive No. 16. It had been delivered to them individually by special messenger from the Planning Group. It was 16 July 1940, the French surrender had been accepted almost a month earlier.

The influence of von Brauchitsch and Halder was fairly obvious in the Directive, and paragraph 1 called for 'a surprise crossing on a broad front extending approximately from Ramsgate to a point west of the Isle of Wight'. There was a suggestion that it might be better to occupy the Isle of Wight or Cornwall before the full-scale invasion.

Paragraph 2 called for the elimination by the Luftwaffe of opposition by the RAF, the laying of impassable mine-fields in the Channel and the pinning down of the Royal Navy in the North Sea and the Mediterranean.

Kästner finished reading first, and he leaned back in his chair, waiting for von Bayer to look up. Five minutes later von Bayer sighed and pushed aside the file cover.

'What do you think of it, Max?'

'Well there's no possibility of it being a surprise landing on a front as wide as that. But the rest of it is no problem. The Luftwaffe have got to knock out the RAF and the Navy have got to get our troops safely across.'

'Any other comments?'

'Yes. I think they ought to be sending recce groups across the Channel. Aerial photographs aren't enough. We should be checking their defences on the ground.'

'You mean raiding parties?'

'No. They could just check certain strategic points. The main landing places and a few diversions so that they can't establish where we shall attack. There's no need for any military action. But our intelligence is getting stale. It's months out of date and after Dunkirk they'll have been preparing for an invasion. We need to know what they have done. An order of battle's not enough and the situation report is more speculation than fact.'

'What size of patrol and how'd you get them over?'

'Five men, six at most. They could be transported by E-boats or subs. Or they could parachute in.'

Kästner looked across at von Bayer for several minutes before he spoke.

'Would you lead such a party yourself?'

'Of course. I'd go tomorrow if I had the chance.'

Kästner nodded. 'I'll see what my people in Berlin have to say. There was a rumour a few days ago that Admiral Raeder was getting cold feet and was putting up problems to the Führer.'

In London, almost unbelievably, nobody had given any thought to the possibility of invasion until the middle of May 1940. Napoleon had failed and the Spanish Armada had failed, and Britain rested on the knowledge that she had not been invaded in nearly 900 years. The country had been ill-prepared for war, and invasion had not even been considered. There was not even an eccentric retired admiral or general who had spent his retirement advocating a counter-invasion plan. Like earthquakes, invasions happened elsewhere. And when France had been obviously crumbling, 'feelers' were still coming from the Germans via Stockholm, Madrid and Lisbon suggesting an accommodation. The 'feelers' had been ignored and it was only then accepted that this open and public contempt for a deal with the German government and its Führer could make invasion a possibility.

In July the RAF had started its bombing raids on Germany. And on the night of 1/2 August the Luftwaffe dropped thousands of leaflets in various parts of England. They were in English, with a headline reading 'A last appeal to reason'. They gave a translation of Hitler's speech in the Reichstag offering peace almost unconditionally. The British public who had read of the offer in the press two weeks before, handed the leaflets to the Red Cross who auctioned them to raise a little money for their funds.

Six hundred and twenty-seven million pounds' worth of gold and 1,250 million pounds' worth of negotiable securities were loaded into boxes addressed to the Sun Life Insurance Company in Montreal and Ottawa. And the Royal Navy cruiser *Emerald* had already landed its cargo of 9,000 gold bars at the port of Halifax.

It was a very hot summer, and all over southern England men sweated as they erected metal hoops over the main roads to prevent them from being used as landing strips by aircraft. In a Kent churchyard they buried arms and ammunition in the graves. And in Chatham, water-tight containers packed with rifles and ammunition were sunk deep into the tidal mud and marked by small buoys. General Sir Alan Brooke, C-in-C Home Forces, noted in his private diary that, of his twenty-two divisions, only about half could be looked on as in any way fit for operations. From the military attaché at the British embassy in Washington came a rumour that the Germans were intending to invade through Devon and Cornwall. Lord Haw-Haw described nightly on the radio the horrifying injuries that would be sustained by the civilians in the landing areas.

Kästner and von Bayer watched the training exercises on the barges and had been horrified at the ineptitude. They waited for the adverse reports to come their way from the command staff of the 16th and 9th Armies. But none came. Kästner sent their own commentary to Berlin but there was neither response nor acknowledgement.

There were situation reports from Raeder's staff on the problems of finding and assembling suitable craft for the crossing and at several meetings von Bayer sat in silent anger as Navy officers derided the whole operation. The Führer's Directive No. 16 had changed the name of the operation to 'Sea-Lion', and Luftwaffe and Navy officers poured scorn on the operation with juvenile jokes about sea-lions.

There had been a special announcement from the Führer's HQ that Reinhard Heydrich was to be the first Reichsprotecktor in Great Britain, and would take over command once the first re-supplies had gone in for the assault units. His initial HQ would be the Spa Hotel in Tunbridge Wells.

Kästner had laughed as he read the announcement and Von Bayer had looked at him.

'Why the joke, Herr Oberst?'

'I think this announcement is a dig in the ribs from the Führer to the Grand-Admiral himself. A little hint to get moving.'

'Why do you think that?'

Kästner was smiling. 'Heydrich was in the Navy once upon a time and Raeder himself threw him out.'

'Why?'

'He's a homosexual. That's no hindrance in the Party, so Raeder will have to watch his step. The Nazis don't like him. Heydrich will be waiting for a chance to square up that old account.'

Even the General Staff appreciations slowly grew more tentative. And two things became clear at all levels. The German Navy, which, in the person of Admiral Raeder, had initiated the operation, were beginning to pass the responsibility on to the Luftwaffe for the success of Sea-Lion. Almost every day there were modifications and amendments to Directive No. 16. But S-Day was finally fixed as 21 September and this would be preceded by the final order from the Führer on 11 September.

By the first week in August the Wehrmacht were moving into the coastal towns of Belgium and France. They were billeted in villages and farms up to fifty kilometres back from the coast and in the deserted seaside villas and hotels at the coast itself. Heavy guns lay under their camouflage nets on railway sidings near Le Havre and the Pas de Calais. Civilians were evacuated from the operational area and new airfields were being hurriedly built to take the fighters and bombers. The civilian population saw the obvious preparations for invasion; and despaired or rejoiced according to their individual prejudices, that Britain was about to take the medicine that they themselves had taken.

Docks and quaysides were being urgently repaired and along the canals and inland waterways barges were moving in one direction only: towards the coast. And the populace tried to avoid looking as formations up to company strength clambered into boats and clambered out again. Day after day and night after night the Luftwaffe planes droned over the coastal towns and villages, heading north across the Channel to England.

Only Field-Marshal Goering and the Luftwaffe staff in Berlin still showed their original enthusiasm, and Operation Eagle was, in Goering's own directive, to start 'the great battle of the German Air Force against England'.

There was a full-scale all-services conference in the first week in August. Raeder, von Brauchitsch and Goering were due to attend. There had been a murmur of acknowledgement as the heads of the three services had walked in, and then a gasp and a clatter of chairs as they stood to attention again as the Führer himself walked into the hall.

They all noted that Hitler had not joined the three commanders at the table but sat at one side alone, gazing into space as Goering addressed them all. The Luftwaffe, he announced, would start Operation Eagle in a matter of days. Their task would be to destroy Fighter Command and its installations in south-eastern England. They would attain complete air-control over the Channel for Operation Sea-Lion. There would be no problems, they were ready and eager to fulfil their role. Von Bayer had watched Raeder's impassive face as his senior planning officer read out a report that was a litany of the problems that the Navy would face in transporting a hundred thousand men across the Channel. Mines, bad weather, high tides, unsuitable vessels, enemy control of the Channel; nothing was left but a silence when he sat down. A silence so long that they could hear the orders being given to troops on the parade ground half a kilometre away. The Army's report outlined accurately, but without comment, what they knew of the British countermeasures in the southern counties. Hitler had listened to the last report with his hand cupped to his ear. Von Bayer made a mental note that in presenting the British order of battle the report had created a spurious armoured brigade in the Croydon area, and an imaginary division to the north of Tunbridge Wells. He glanced at Kästner's face, but it was impassive as he listened.

Outside on the parade ground the Führer presented Knight's Crosses and Iron Crosses to members of all three services, and von Bayer felt a burning anger at the apathetic attitude of the Navy and the Army. Goering, the old comrade from the days of Munich, was the only enthusiast among them. No wonder the Führer was rumoured to despise the Supreme Command and to rely only on the Nazis. Maybe he was right. It was the professional soldiers who had advised against marching into Vienna and Prague, and the attack on Poland. When somebody took the responsibility and told them what to do, they did it well, but they had no courage of conviction. It was Hitler who had always had that courage.

Kästner invited him to walk along the bank of the canal that led to Sluis and they sat at the edge of a field, eating peas from the crop.

'Well, what did you think about that, my boy?'

'They're gutless, Colonel. And we are losing time. We should have gone straight over after Dunkirk before they had time to regroup and recover.'

'What do you think will happen now?'

'The Luftwaffe will do its job and the others will be forced to follow.'

Kästner threw an empty pea-pod on to the water and watched as it was nudged by a pike.

'Are you a Nazi, Max?'

'I told you that I'm not a member of the Party.'

'I know. But do you support Hitler?'

'Every inch of the way.'

'Why?'

'Even I can remember when a newspaper cost a thousand million marks, and one-legged ex-soldiers were begging in the streets, and Berlin was full of queers. Hitler has put an end to all that. The French and the British tried to keep us in the gutter with the Versailles Treaty. We were made to promise to pay them more money than there was in the world. They asked for trouble, and now they're going to get it. When the English are defeated we are all square. Maybe we can start again.'

Kästner looked at von Bayer's angry face. 'Generals never trust politicians, and history has proved them right.'

'Hitler's more than a politician. He's a leader. A real leader. He has done more for Germany in eight years than anybody else has done in a century.'

Kästner smiled. 'Do you think Sea-Lion is workable?'

'Of course. The Luftwaffe wipes out Fighter Command and the rest is an exercise.'

'And the British Army?'

'Without air cover they don't stand a chance.'

Kästner stood up. 'Let's get back to the grind.'

On 8 August the Luftwaffe threw down its challenge to RAF Fighter Command – 'Come up and fight if you dare'. Fighter Command dared, but it had no intention of being wiped out piecemeal in old-fashioned dog-fights. And day after day the RAF's radar, and Fighter Command's efficient control systems had kept the rate of attrition marginally balanced in favour of the RAF.

Coastal Command and reconnaissance sorties showed barges and other craft being assembled along the coast and in the harbours of France, Belgium and Holland; and they were attacked with incendiary bombs day after day.

By 24 August the Luftwaffe was concentrating its attacks on Fighter Command's airfields and sector stations, and now the Spitfires and Hurricanes were having to come up to defend their nests. By 6 September Fighter Command was in serious trouble. In fourteen days it had lost 295 fighters, totally destroyed, 171 seriously damaged, and the replacements had been only 269: 300 experienced pilots had been lost against only 260 new fledglings from the flying schools. The balance was beginning to tilt fatally in the Luftwaffe's favour.

Air Chief Marshal Sir Hugh Dowding, C-in-C Fighter Command, decided that if losses continued at the same rate for another three days he would withdraw his remaining fighters to the north of England no matter what destruction the Luftwaffe's bombers wreaked on the undefended towns of southern England.

Six

The twenty-third of August was one of Berlin's hottest days that summer, and the motorized Wehrmacht unit stood sweating in the glaring afternoon sun at Templehof airfield. There were two limousines drawn up alongside the terminal buildings and six BMW motor-cycles were propped up on their rear-wheel stands.

The runways had been cleared of all aircraft, and the twin-engined Cessna landed smoothly and taxied past the normal control area to the terminal building itself. Ribbentrop's personal assistant walked towards the man who climbed down from the small aircraft.

The two men got in the big black Mercedes and the second car and the escort motor-cyclists fell in behind. The party left from the gates used for freight, and when the first Mercedes pulled up at the Chancery steps neither the second car nor the motor-cycle escort were in view.

Lincoln Ames was the United States Ambassador to Portugal. Comfortably off, but not rich, from the family fortune made by shrewd investments that had survived the slump. He had practised law in Washington before he had been recommended to Roosevelt as the man he needed in London. But in the end Joe Kennedy had gone to London and Ames to Lisbon. A posting that overnight had gone from being a quiet backwater to the centre of espionage and the source of most rumours from both sides. It was also the neutral trading post for both Germany and Britain. When he had been recalled to Washington he half-expected that the

47

President was going to oust him in favour of a Democrat. Whatever his guesses might have been he knew that he could never have conjured up the task the President had actually given him.

There had been no discussion about what he had to say to the German Reichskanzler, he was told exactly what he had to say, with the answers to some obvious supplementary questions that might be asked. His opinion had not been invited on the message he was to carry. He was told that he had been chosen because he could be trusted, because he spoke fluent German, and because his face was virtually unknown to both the American press and the foreign press.

The Secretary of State had rehearsed him again and again and he had signed a piece of White House stationery that warned him of the dire consequences if he ever talked. He was to say no more than he was told to say, and he was to report back with his impressions of Hitler's reaction. The United States Ambassador in Berlin would have no knowledge that he was in Berlin, and would not be so informed by Washington. He was not to stay overnight in Berlin unless the Germans wished him to return with an answer, or they forcibly detained him. The Germans had given an undertaking regarding his safe-conduct, but that was not necessarily to be relied on.

The Germans kept him waiting for three hours in a small bare room. They brought him coffee and a copy of the previous week's *New Yorker*. It was early evening when the Foreign Minister's personal assistant came for him, and they walked briskly down a dim side corridor to an office marked with only a number: 701.

It was obviously not Hitler's office or even von Ribbentrop's, but it was impressive enough with its mahogany panelling and crystal chandeliers.

He was shown to a seat facing a massive desk that was empty of papers except for a blank pad and three pencils. A solitary oil-painting of Bismarck hung on the wall behind the desk. Otherwise the room was without decoration.

A door in the far corner opened and an official stood to one side as Hitler and von Ribbentrop came into the room.

48

Without even glancing towards Ames, the Führer sat down in the centre chair, with von Ribbentrop alongside him. It was von Ribbentrop who spoke.

'Say what you have to say, Herr Ames.'

'I have been instructed to deliver my message to the German Chancellor without any other person present.'

'I will act as interpreter.'

'No, Your Excellency. I speak German.'

Hitler obviously understood, and without hesitating he nodded to von Ribbentrop to leave. Ames saw von Ribbentrop's face flush with anger as he strode to the door. When the door closed behind him, Hitler nodded.

'So, Herr Ames. *Fangen Sie bitte an.*'

Slowly and precisely Ames gave him the personal message from the President of the United States that said that if the German Forces or their allies invaded Great Britain, or landed forces on British soil, then the United States of America would declare war on Germany in the following twenty-four hours.

The German Chancellor sat there in his grey jacket and dark blue tie, his face impassive but his dark eyes on Ames' face. Then Hitler spoke, his voice quite even and controlled.

'Have the press been informed of this message?'

'Only three people know of the message, Your Excellency. Four with yourself.'

'Who are the others?'

'The President, the Secretary of State and myself.'

'And Churchill?'

'No, Your Excellency, the Prime Minister has not been informed.'

'Do you expect an answer, Herr Ames?'

'No, Your Excellency. I am instructed only to deliver the private message. But I would take back a reply if you so wished.'

The German Chancellor stood up, and, without any acknowledgement to Ames, walked out of the room.

An amiable von Ribbentrop came in a few minutes later. They would have a meal together in private, and afterwards the Foreign Minister himself would drive him to the airport.

As they ate it was obvious that Hitler had not informed von Ribbentrop of the contents of the message, and not over-subtly von Ribbentrop tried to ferret out the contents as they talked. Ames carried out his instructions to the letter. He did not discuss the message or even try to give a false impression of what its subject matter might be.

When the operational orders for the Luftwaffe's Operation Eagle were discussed, the classification of targets for the bombers was precise. The Luftwaffe would confine its bombing raids to Fighter Command airfields, sector controls, regional controls, RAF radar and communications installations, and aircraft manufacturing plants. Hitler himself had given a direct order that London would not be bombed.

On the night of 4 September a Dornier was hit over RAF Manston, and, almost out of control, it banked in a big circle to try to get back to the coast. Losing height rapidly it released its bombs in a vain attempt to gain altitude, and eventually crashed near Reading. Its bomb load fell on Lambeth. Although neither its crew nor anyone else could have imagined it at the time, their bombs were probably the turning point of the war.

In anger, Winston Churchill ordered Bomber Command to bomb Berlin for the first time the following day. When the bombs fell on Berlin the city was stunned. Hermann Goering and Adolf Hitler had said that British bombs would never fall on the capital of the Third Reich.

On 7 September the Luftwaffe mounted a massive night attack on London. It was the start of the Blitz and night after night the Luftwaffe had pounded the capital. And day after day Fighter Command could not believe the miracle. With only a handful of serviceable fighters left to defend the whole country they were being given respite to repair, build and reorganize their tattered forces. London's sacrifice and Goering's vanity were giving them the breathing space they needed. There were those who said later that it was the hand of God. But they said it with hindsight, and none of them was a Londoner.

Von Bayer was given leave for the second week in September, and he declined it because it was too near the day when Hitler would give the final orders for Sea-Lion to go into action. He would issue the final order on the fourteenth and the Navy would start laying the mines, and the barges would assemble at their final ports of departure. Units would get their detailed orders, and maps and handbooks would be issued.

Von Bayer waited impatiently on the fourteenth for his copy of the directive, and grew angrier as the hours went by.

It was 4 p.m. when the signals motor-cyclist delivered the big grey envelopes for himself and Kästner. Kästner sat at his desk, his envelope unopened as he watched von Bayer impatiently tear open his packet. He stood reading the single sheet of paper and then looked up, white-faced, and incredulous.

'You'll never guess, Otto. You'll never guess.'

Kästner looked back at him. 'Sea-Lion has been postponed.'

'How the hell did you know?'

'I didn't *know*. But it was obvious.'

'But why?'

'The Luftwaffe failed to defeat the RAF. The Navy are shit-scared of making the crossing. That adds up to postponement. And in two or three weeks' time we shall all be going back to our regular units.'

'I don't believe it.'

Kästner shrugged. 'The RAF have given Goering and his boys a bloody nose. Raeder never wanted the crossing from the start, and the Wehrmacht are sitting like Christ knows what in their barges. Those bloody barges couldn't cross a park lake.'

'So why didn't they assemble suitable craft?'

'Maybe they didn't want to. They may not *have* suitable craft anyway.'

'But Hitler gave them direct orders. He is their Commander-in-Chief.'

'He'll get his revenge on them eventually, but he isn't going to get Operation Sea-Lion. I'll bet on that.'

'The bastards. The cowardly bastards.'

Von Bayer crushed the paper into a ball and slung it away as he stormed out of the room.

The next day RAF fighter pilots shot down sixty German aircraft for the loss of only twenty-six RAF fighters, and Bomber Command rained bombs on the assembled invasion barges on the French coast. Burned corpses in German uniforms were washed up on the Kent coast and rumours started in southern England of an invasion attempt that had been made and beaten back. The British authorities did nothing to stop the rumours or deny them. The Chiefs of Staff Committee reported to Churchill that day, that with the autumn fogs around 19 October there could still be suitable invasion days.

In the week following 14 September von Bayer haunted the planning sections, collecting reports and maps, details of targets and tides, background material and documentation. Kästner joked about the battered wooden tea-case that contained von Bayer's collection.

The twenty-first of September was yet another hot day, and von Bayer drove to the coast to Ostend. The sea was flat and calm. It was to have been the start day of 'Sea-Lion'. It would have been a perfect day for an invasion fleet, and the fleccy white clouds in the blue sky augured well for the weather in the next few days. He went to the cinema in the Rue Longue. It was Leni Riefenstahl's film of the 1936 Olympics. It all seemed a long, long time ago. He had a meal afterwards in one of the back-street hotels, and was back in Bruges at ten o'clock. It was already dark, and the canals stank from the summer heat.

There was a note on his bed from Kästner. It said he had been given eight weeks' leave. He rushed into Kästner's bedroom before he realized that there was a girl in bed with Kästner. But the Abwehr colonel was not embarrassed.

'What is it, Max?'

Von Bayer waved the note. 'This. Why?'

'We've *all* got eight weeks' leave. The operation is off.

"Indefinitely postponed" is the official version. The fact is, the party's over.'

'But why eight weeks?'

Kästner grinned. 'It's long enough for us all to forget what we've been doing. I recommend that you *do* forget. All of it.'

Von Bayer closed the door behind him and went slowly back to his room.

The next day he packed his kit and went for his travel warrant and leave pass. The planning offices were empty except for the movement-control staff who issued him his documents.

Kästner was standing in the sunshine on the steps of the house when he got back.

'Can I speak to you, Colonel?'

'Of course. But my advice is, don't do it.'

Von Bayer looked surprised. 'But you don't know what I had in mind?'

'Oh but I do, my friend. It's been written all over your face for several weeks. Especially this last week.'

'Tell me,' von Bayer said softly.

'You'd be crazy to talk about it here. D'you remember the place on the canal where we ate the peas?'

'Yes.'

'I'll see you there in an hour.'

Kästner arrived late carrying two leather cases. When he was sitting beside him he turned and looked at von Bayer's grim face.

'So talk, Sturmbannführer.'

'You said you already know.'

Kästner shrugged. 'After the failure of the Luftwaffe to deliver, and the Navy to get started, our hero Maximilian von Bayer is going to swim the Channel and beard the enemy in his lair. Or words to that effect.'

'Not just me. I would find others.'

'You know what *you* need, Max?'

'What?'

'A nice girl. Or better still a nasty girl. But a very pretty, nasty girl, who'll let you screw her for eight weeks.'

'With a handful of men I could do more damage in a few weeks than the Luftwaffe did in Operation Eagle.'

'Maybe you could. But why should you?'

'To show those bastards that it could have been done.'

'What do you want, a Knight's Cross? I can get you one of those in a week.'

'They're going to throw it all away. All that the Führer has gained for us. He gives them orders to do something and they just say that it isn't possible. They didn't send a single recce party over. They didn't test the defences. They relied on photographs and gossip. The bastards didn't make even the elementary moves.'

'And what could you and your gang do?'

'Destroy aircraft on the ground. Destroy their radar stations. Destroy their control centres.'

Kästner looked across the canal, his hand tugging idly at the grass beside him.

'You know, Sturmbannführer, you may be right. If your operation worked there could be a dozen such operations. Bigger ones. Maybe that's what we ought to have done first and then sent the real stuff over later.'

'Will you help me?'

'Help you do what?'

'Find the men and train them.'

'The authorities would never agree, Max.'

'I don't intend to ask them.'

'Tell me more.'

'I'll find experts who are civilians, or ex-service people who have been wounded but are still mobile. It will be entirely unofficial.'

'And you yourself?'

'I'll desert at the end of my leave.'

'Jesus Christ, they'd shoot you when they caught you.'

'Not if I succeed. And I shall. It'll be good training.'

'Tell me. What would your targets be?'

'The radar stations at Rye and Lympne. The fighter

stations at Tangmere and West Malling and the sector control at Biggin Hill. Anything that we could get at.'

'And who pays for this enterprise, or do you live off the land?'

'I'll pay. And we'll live off the land.'

Kästner looked back at him. 'D'you really mean to do this?'

'I swear it.'

Kästner looked across the canal, over the flat Belgian fields to where an ME-109 was doing a slow victory roll before it landed at the airfield due north of the town. It was a long time before Kästner spoke again. He turned to look at von Bayer.

'We could use you in the Abwehr, Max. I would guarantee you immediate promotion.'

Von Bayer half-smiled and shrugged. 'Thanks, Otto. But this has got to be done.'

Kästner nodded and sighed. 'It's crazy, and it's doomed. One side of the Channel or the other. But I understand. You'd better keep in touch if you want help.'

'Where will you be?'

'In Berlin. My telephone number's in the book.'

They walked back together to the town, and von Bayer carried one of Kästner's bags as far as the railway station. Kästner didn't look back as he walked through the gates to the platform.

Von Bayer slept solidly for twelve hours after he arrived back at Schloss Eger. In the evening when he went down to see his father there was a message for him. Someone had phoned him from Berlin and left a number for him to ring.

It was Kästner and he was very brief. He suggested that von Bayer should see him in Berlin as soon as possible. He wouldn't give any reason or explanation, and von Bayer agreed to travel up to see him the next day.

Kästner's apartment was in one of the streets off the Kurfürstendamm. Expensively furnished, so that von Bayer suddenly realized how little he knew of Kästner's background or circumstances. But there was no doubt that he

55

could not maintain a place like this solely on a colonel's pay. Kästner took him into a study where several files were laid out on a mahogany table. There was a map of Germany at one end of the table and at the other end a map of south-east England. There were two high-backed chairs on the same side of the table and Kästner pointed to one of them.

'Sit down, Max.'

Kästner took the other chair and reached across to pull the map of England in front of them. Then he looked at von Bayer.

'Have you thought any more about your crazy scheme? Have you thought better of it?'

'I've thought a lot about it, Otto. And I've not thought better of it.'

'Tell me what you've been thinking.'

'I've been thinking about the kind of men I'll need.'

'Tell me.'

Von Bayer shook his head. 'I'm going to need tight security, Otto. It's best you don't know anything.'

Kästner looked at him half-smiling. 'You're going to need a lot of help, my boy.'

'Are you offering to help me?'

'Maybe.'

'What kind of help?'

Kästner smiled. 'Let's hear a bit more and then we'll talk.' He nodded towards the map. 'Where do you intend to land?'

Von Bayer hesitated for a moment and then looked at the map. He pointed with his finger.

'Somewhere here, between Camber and St Mary's Bay. I've got photographs of all this coast.'

'And what are your targets going to be?'

'I haven't finally decided, but there are half a dozen airfields that I can cover, and there are the radar towers at Rye and Lympne.'

'And the men. What do you need?'

'Experts on radio, explosives, demolition, a sniper, a first-class mechanic, an armourer and an armoured vehicle man. Maybe a driver and a cook.'

'Where are you going to find them?'

'I don't know yet.'

'Maybe I can find them for you. I've got two names already.'

Von Bayer was silent as he looked at the map. Then he said quietly. 'Do I have your word of honour that you will mention this to nobody?'

'Yes.'

'Isn't this dangerous for you?'

'If you fail it will be dangerous. Or if they discover what you're doing before you go.'

'I wouldn't give them your name, Otto.'

Kästner smiled. 'You'd talk, Max. Everybody does. In the end.'

Von Bayer looked at Kästner's face. 'Why are you doing this, Otto?'

Kästner sighed, half-smiling. 'God knows. Partly because I admire your courage, and partly because I'm technically interested in how you get on. And, I suppose, partly because I think you're right.'

'And do you think I'll succeed?'

'Oddly enough, I do.'

'Tell me about the two men.'

'One was a sabotage and demolition officer attached to a Panzer unit, and the other was a White Hunter in Kenya.'

'How did you find them?'

'I knew them both already. I felt they might be what you wanted.'

'When can I see them?'

'One is in Berlin. You could see him today. The other lives in Hamburg. You'd have to see him there.'

'What do you think their reaction will be?'

'They're crazy bastards. I'm sure that they'll both jump at the chance. I'll act as a reference point for your seriousness if you wish. Here are their names and addresses.'

He pushed across a slip of paper and von Bayer read it carefully, slid it into his pocket and stood up.

'Tell me about them.'

'No. You form your own opinion, Max. Everything's

going to stand or fall on making the right choice. My choice might not be yours.'

'I'd better find a bed for the night.'

'The SS get special rates at the Adlon.'

Von Bayer smiled. 'Sure, and when they come looking for me that's the first place they'll check.'

Kästner grinned. *'Hals- und Beinbruch!'*

'Hals- und Beinbruch!'

Seven

It was an old-fashioned looking house but it had obviously been built sometime at the turn of the century when land was still cheap enough in the fine Berlin suburb of Tiergarten to afford a good-sized garden.

There were full-blown roses round the porch, and geraniums in a hanging wire basket. The lawns were trim and sharp-edged, and the borders were thick with Michaelmas daisies, sunflowers and sweet-scented stocks.

He walked up the flagstones to the porch and pressed the bell. An old lady in black answered the door and when he asked for Herr Voss she nodded silently and opened the door wide for him to walk into the hall. She pointed, without speaking, to a chair and he sat down.

There was a faint smell of cooking from the back of the house and a radio news-bulletin was announcing that British and so-called Free French forces had attempted, and failed, to neutralize the French fleet at Dakar. Von Bayer found it difficult to decide whether the house was peaceful or merely gloomy. The stillness gave an empty air to the place. Then suddenly a tall, thin man was standing beside him, looking at him. Von Bayer realised that the man must have come down the stairs without making a sound.

The man put out his hand.

'Erich Voss, let's go in my study.'

The room was panelled in dark wood to the height of about a metre, and the rest of the walls were white. No pictures, no ornament of any kind. Noticing von Bayer's examination of the room Voss smiled and said, 'Are you looking for the heads of lion and kudu?'

'I suppose I was, subconsciously.' Von Bayer smiled.

'Those are for the amateurs. I guess I don't have to prove anything any more.'

'Did you like your job in Kenya?'

'Sometimes. The job paid for me to do what I would have done anyway.'

'What made you come back?'

Voss smiled. 'I saw the English vultures circling round, and left early in August. They would have interned me if I had stayed.'

'What do you do now?'

Voss shrugged and grinned. 'I value sporting guns for four or five gunsmiths. I teach fieldcraft to Wehrmacht instructors. I've just written the OKW handbook on sniping. I've designed a night-sight, telescopic, that I hope the army will buy.' He sniffed dismissively. 'I've made enough to live on for a long time, my friend.'

'Did Otto Kästner mention what I was going to talk about?'

'He certainly did. We're old friends, Kästner and I. He's a shrewd man is Otto. He knew I'd want to go.'

'Do you want to join my team?'

'You bet.'

'You know what I intend doing, and where?'

'Yes. On both counts. That's all OK by me.'

'You speak good English.'

'Yes. I worked there for three years and I had ten years in Kenya.'

'Are you married, Herr Voss?'

'No. And no dependants. I'm free as a bird.'

'Could you make your own way to my home at Schloss Eger?'

'Of course. When do you want me there?'

'Say in three days' time?'

'Fine. I'll bring two guns and a couple of hand guns.'

It was one of the old houses near the Goose Market, and von

Bayer stood on the top step looking round after he had pressed the bell that said KLEIST W. For the first time he actually saw a bombed building. He had heard that there had been two raids on Hamburg but he hadn't yet got used to connecting air-raids with bombed houses. Not in Germany.

Then the door opened, and a man came out carrying a briefcase. He hesitated as he made to close the door.

'Are you calling on someone?'

'I rang the bell for Herr Kleist.'

The man shook his head. 'You won't find him here at this time of night. He'll be at the club.'

'What club is that?'

The man frowned, trying to recall the name. 'A tree. The name of a tree. God, what is it? Not a big tree. *Die Linde*. That's it. The Linden.'

'Could you tell me where it is?'

'You know the Vier Jahreszeiten?'

'Yes.'

'In the street at the back. There's a sign. It's a basement, next to a piano showroom that's been taken over by the *Winterhilfs* people.'

It was early for a night-club, and fewer than half the tables were occupied. The man at the cloakroom asked him if he was a member and he had been nodded in when he showed his SS identity card. The man had given him a cursory glance and taken his raincoat.

'Can you tell me where I can find Herr Kleist?'

'He'll be playing right now. He's the resident pianist.'

Von Bayer stood at the top of the carpeted steps that led down to the dance floor and the two rows of tables. The boudoir grand was a Bechstein and the man playing it was improvising as he talked to a girl who was leaning on the top of the piano listening to what he was saying. His left hand played idle chords as his right hand reached out and took one of the girl's hands as she bent to kiss him. Then both his hands were back on the piano as he softly led into the opening chords of a song that von Bayer faintly remembered. A few of the couples clapped and the girl stood up and looked over her shoulder smiling towards the tables. A man shouted something, and the girl nodded, and reached for the microphone on its heavy stand.

She turned to look affectionately at the pianist, then she sang, and the room was still. A spotlight moved to her face and von Bayer saw that she was exceptionally beautiful. And as he listened he was moved, not only by the girl, but her voice, and the words that she sang – '*Ich schenk' mein Herz nur einem Mann, dem ich in Liebe treu sein kann* ... I give my heart just to one man.' She sang effortlessly, her voice full and clear and she sang as if she meant every word.

The waiters stood in a group alongside him listening silently until the song had ended. The applause was spontaneous and enthusiastic. She blew a kiss to the man at the piano and walked over to join a couple at one of the tables.

Von Bayer walked down the steps and over to the small bar. He ordered a drink and when the barman put it in front of him he said, 'What's the pianist's favourite drink?'

'He doesn't drink, sir. Maybe a tomato juice. He brings a bottle of milk for himself most nights. He's got some stomach trouble. Been wounded I think. In Poland. Here's the one who'll know.'

It was the girl and she smiled at the barman.

'What are you up to, Albert?'

'Gentleman wanted to buy a drink for Herr Kleist. I told him he didn't drink.'

The girl turned to look at von Bayer. She was so beautiful that he was suddenly at a loss for words.

'Do you know Walter?' she asked, smiling.

'I've got an introduction to him, and I liked his playing. I liked your singing too. It was very moving.'

Suddenly the blue eyes were really looking at him. 'An odd word – moving – to hear in a night-club. Nice. Do you want to meet Walter?'

'I should like to.'

She walked across the small dancing area and leaned over the piano. He saw Kleist look towards him, and a few moments later he stood up and walked over towards the bar.

He had a pronounced limp in his left leg. He was tall and slim, and he looked at home in evening dress. He was a handsome man with a lean, gentle face, and as he approached von Bayer he held out his hand, smiling.

'I'm glad you liked Ushi's song. She sings beautifully when we can persuade her to perform.'

Von Bayer took his hand. 'I've come from Otto Kästner, I hope this is not too inconvenient.'

The mouth still smiled, but not the eyes. 'Ah, yes. I'll get my coat, and we'll take a little walk. I need a breath of fresh air.'

He walked awkwardly up the stairs. 'My coat, Heinz. Tell Kurt I'm having a breather outside for about ten minutes.'

Kleist slid his coat loosely across his shoulders and led the way up to the street.

The black-out was complete and it took time before their eyes were adjusted. Kleist walked slowly until they were alongside the big inland harbour of the Binnenalster. A trio of searchlights were probing slowly across the night sky, but there had been no air-raid alarm.

'Does walking hurt your leg?'

'No. The contrary. It's sitting that makes me limp. It cuts off the circulation. Don't worry about that. It soon goes.'

'What did Otto tell you?'

Von Bayer's eyes had adjusted to the moonlight and he saw Kleist smiling.

'Enough my friend. I think it's a great scheme. It'll be like old times for me.'

'You mean you're willing to join me?'

'You bet. I wouldn't miss it for the world. Mind you I've got a problem.'

'What's that?'

'It's not a what, it's a who. Ushi.'

'The girl who sang?'

'Yes.'

'Why is she a problem?'

'How long d'you reckon we'd be away?'

'Until we've done the job.'

'I know, but roughly how long?'

'God knows, a month, two months maybe.'

'Yes. That's the problem.'

'Tell me.'

'Ushi loves me. She'd hate me being away.'

'Do you love *her*?'

'Not quite the same way. I can't afford to. But I owe too much to Ushi to hurt her even for an hour.'

'I don't understand.'

'Of course not. When I got hit they didn't really expect me to live. They released me from hospital so that I could go off quietly somewhere and die. Ushi took me over, and I'm alive. Entirely because of what she did for me. It wasn't very pleasant for her I can tell you. It still isn't. She's an angel. You see?'

'You said you couldn't afford to love her. Why not?'

'It's rather embarrassing, old chap.'

'Try me.'

'I won't last more than another six months at the outside. She doesn't know that. But I owe her every minute of the time I've got left.'

Von Bayer looked at the handsome face. The eyes were smiling. 'You do love her, don't you?'

'Oh yes. But it would be unfair to tell her so.'

'What time do you finish tonight?'

'We have to close at midnight. It's the law.'

'I'm booked in at the Adlon, could we meet there after you've finished, or will you be too tired by then?'

'Sure we can. I'm fit really, you know.'

Von Bayer walked back in the darkness to the Adlon, thinking of the man who said he was fit. Except for whatever would kill him in the next six months. Kleist had all the air of a typical Berlin playboy. But you don't get a Knight's Cross and invalided out of a Panzer unit just for your charm.

It was nearly one in the morning when the reception desk at the Adlon phoned up to his room to say that Herr Kleist had arrived. He asked them to send him up.

Von Bayer went out into the corridor and walked to the lift gates. He was disappointed and slightly annoyed when he saw that Kleist had brought the girl along with him. That would mean that they couldn't talk.

Back in his room he telephoned the night porter for coffee.

Kleist sat on the old-fashioned settee, holding the girl's hand, his eyes alight with enthusiasm.

'I've had a wonderful idea, von Bayer. We'll take Ushi with us. Part of the team.'

Von Bayer avoided the girl's eyes. 'We can't do that, Kleist. There'll only be six of us. We'll all be specialists with a definite role to play.'

'You're going to need a radio operator, yes?'

'Yes.'

Kleist smiled and patted the girl's knee. 'This lovely creature is a radio technician. It's her job. She's fully trained. Works for Radio Hamburg.'

Von Bayer looked at the girl. 'Tell me what you do.'

She shrugged. 'I was trained at the Technische Hochschule and when I qualified I went straight to Radio Hamburg. I'm deputy in charge of all technical equipment.'

'Can you operate a military set? Can you read Morse?'

'You do that in your first year. I can operate any transmitter provided I see the manual. I can read and transmit Morse to a higher standard than Wehrmacht signals call for.'

'What about your job?'

She grinned. 'Maybe I have to become pregnant.'

'This isn't a joy-ride. Not even just a tough journey. It isn't girl's work.'

'There are girls manning anti-aircraft guns, and nurses with fighting units. There haven't been any complaints about them.'

The couple sat there with their eyes on his face waiting for his answer. It went through his mind that they were like a couple asking permission to marry. He must have looked like that to Moshe Aarons.

He looked at both of them. 'Are you sure you want to do this. Both of you?'

Kleist nodded. 'Provided you want us.'

Suddenly von Bayer's doubts were dispelled. He grinned.

'It's so crazy it might work. When can you both pull out?'

'It would take Ushi two days. I could come right now.'

'Could you both make your way to my home as soon as you can?'

'Of course.'

He gave them directions for finding Schloss Eger, and Kästner's telephone number for simple messages. And they sat talking for an hour as von Bayer outlined some of what had happened on Sea-Lion and what roughly he intended to do.

Back in Berlin he told Kästner of his experiences in Hamburg. He was adamant when Kästner objected strongly to him including the girl.

'It's crazy, Max. You've got five or six men, under stress, in enemy territory. No access to other women, under tension all the while. You've just bought yourself a load of trouble.'

'You know that Walter Kleist only has months to live?'

'No, I didn't know that. But it makes no difference. You'll have trouble. Anyway, it looks like that's water under the bridge. I've found you your demolition man and your vehicle man.'

'How did you find them?'

'One of them, the demolition fellow, I got out of the Gestapo records. They were checking how he managed to stay out of the armed forces. The investigation isn't completed so you've got a pressure point. It looks like he's been paying somebody to keep him out of the army. The vehicle chap was investigated by my people six months ago. Suspected of malingering to avoid service. He isn't malingering. He's got bad lungs, and he's undersize. And in fact he's dying to get in the army.'

'Any messages or mail for me?'

'It's over there on my desk.'

There was the official confirmation of his leave, and the Berlin address where he was to report when his leave was up on 24 November. Ration cards and clothing coupons were enclosed. There was a note from his father. He had been made a *Wehrwirtschaftsführer* in recognition of his services to the Party. There was a bill from his tailor in Brunswick, and then he noticed the pale mauve envelope. It was covered with Field Post Office stamps and several censorship stamps. It was post-marked Cambridge, and the date of posting was over a year ago. He opened it slowly.

He read the brief note a dozen times. It was so typical of her that it was as if she were in the room with him. It had been posted on 1 September 1939, and it was amazing that it had got through and finally caught up with him. She would have been home for the holidays, and had probably sat at the oak table in their sitting-room, the fruit bowl pushed aside, her fingers fiddling with the cap of her fountain-pen. He had always thought musicians had long slender fingers, but hers were strong fingers and there were callouses on the fingertips of her left hand from the strings of her 'cello. He pushed the note back in its envelope, and the envelope into his pocket. She seemed so far away. She might even have been in London when it was being bombed by the Luftwaffe. It seemed incredible that he was planning to be in England in a few weeks' time. He shivered and walked over to the window. He didn't look out. He closed his eyes. He would try the other two men and then he must get down to Schloss Eger and start the detailed planning.

There were two big gates and a painted notice that said '*Gebrüder Schultz*' – *das Sprengkommando*. Schultz Brothers – the demolition commando. There was a small door set in one of the big gates and von Bayer opened it and ducked inside.

A cobbled yard was piled with used bricks, timber, doors, fireplaces, lead piping, glass and window-frames. In the far corner was a small wooden shack. It said 'Office' on the door, and a telephone line sagged across to it from an adjoining building. When he was a few paces away from the office a man came out. Young, red-faced, his grey shirt-sleeves rolled up, and a leather band strapped round one thick wrist. His eyebrows were raised in aggressive query.

'What can I do for you, mister?'

'I'm looking for Otto Schultz.'

'You've found him.'

'Is there anywhere we could talk privately?'

Schultz nodded his head towards the shack, and turned and walked back towards it.

There was a street map of Berlin pinned to the wall, a wooden filing cabinet, and a desk piled untidily with papers. An office swivel-chair with arms was alongside the desk and Schultz sat in it, pointing to the desk.

'Shift the papers.'

Von Bayer sensed the constant aggressive defensiveness of the man and found it vaguely irritating. His Berlin accent was over-harsh, and tinged with permanent resentment. Maybe a frontal attack would be the best approach.

'I understand you've got a problem, Herr Schultz.'

'First I've heard of it, mate.'

'Maybe you don't reckon that the Gestapo are a problem.'

Von Bayer saw the man's eyes narrow and the big fist on the table clench tightly.

'Are you Gestapo?'

'How old are you, Schultz?'

'Twenty-nine.'

'Why aren't you in one of the services?'

Schultz shrugged. 'I've been deferred. They need me to demolish the bombed houses.'

'What government department gives you work?'

'It's not the government. It's Berlin City Council work. Dr Ingenieur Rolf.'

'What car do you run?'

'A little DKW.'

'Whose is the black Merc in the yard?'

'My brother's.'

'What does he do?'

'He's in charge of finances. I just do the demolition.'

'Why don't you have a Merc?'

'Waste of money, mister. Snobs' cars. I could buy my brother out any time I wanted.'

'Are you married?'

Schultz laughed. 'Are you crazy? I get all I want without taking out a long lease.'

'How long does your deferment last?'

'Another two months.'

'Would you be interested in a deal that gave you a permanent deferment?'

Schultz grinned. 'Don't try and trap me, mate. Who are you anyway?'

Von Bayer slid his hand inside his jacket, pulled out his identity card, and holding it in his hand, showed it to Schultz. He read it slowly and carefully, and then looked up at von Bayer's face.

'I don't understand. What's going on?'

'I want to borrow you for a few weeks, Herr Schultz.'

'You mean hire one of my teams?'

'No. I meant what I said. I want to borrow *you* for something special. It's dangerous, and if you said you would be scared I would accept that as a reason.'

Schultz shook his head to demonstrate slow bewilderment.

'I ain't ever been scared in all my life, my friend.'

'Then you're just the man I want.'

'Is this some SS thing?'

'In a way. It's unofficial, but if we succeed your contribution will be recognized.'

'Who's we?'

'You. Me. And four others.'

Von Bayer could see that Schultz was both intrigued and well aware of the benefits of official recognition. And he was aware of other things too.

'How about the people in Prinz Albrechtstrasse?'

'You'll just be away for a few weeks. After you're back, there won't be a problem.'

'When do we start?'

'How long will you need to hand over?'

'I've got two good foremen. A couple of hours.'

'I meant it when I said it was dangerous.'

Schultz grinned. 'I reckon I can show the SS a thing or two, my friend.'

Von Bayer gave Schultz Kästner's address, and warned

him not to tell anybody, including his brother, about what he had been told. Schultz looked the kind of man who would enjoy knowing what others didn't know.

Rudi Kruger lived in the Wedding district in one of the blocks of small apartments built by the Berlin City Council for workers. He answered the door himself because his wife was out at work. He was twenty-four and had been a garage mechanic until the outbreak of war. Now he worked as a free-lance. Much in demand because his bad chest made him unlikely to be called up. Most of his time he worked in the vehicle park of the SS Leibstandarte, Sepp Dietrich's crack SS division that was sorting itself out after the Polish campaign and the dash across Holland to be in at the kill in Paris.

Rudi Kruger lived and breathed internal combustion engines, working long hours for little money. He worshipped the heroes of the Leibstandarte and the walls of his small living-room were covered with photographs of SS Oberst Gruppenführer Dietrich, and the men who served under him. In pride of place was a Leibstandarte cuff title, in a small glass frame.

Von Bayer talked for only ten minutes to Kruger before he knew that he would be an ideal recruit. When he got to the point he was embarrassed by the young man's eagerness. He wanted no details. If it was to work for an SS officer, on vehicles, that was all he wanted to know. He would tell his wife that he was spending a few weeks at the SS driving school in Munich. He had been there several times.

When von Bayer was on his way back to Kästner's flat he was aware that the four men and the girl were now his responsibility entirely. Only partially aware of what was being asked of them, and probably with the impression that their extraordinary project had the blessing of the authorities, despite the secrecy.

He phoned his father, at his Berlin flat and arranged to see him for dinner that evening. Kästner was going to take Schultz and Kruger in hand.

'Why no uniform?'

'I'm on leave, Father.'

'My God, boy, if I were a Sturmbannführer in the SS I should be wearing my number one kit all the time. By the way, old Helmut phoned from Schloss Eger. Seems there are some friends of yours waiting for you. Two fellows and a girl.'

'I should have told you, Father. It slipped my mind.'

'Not to worry. Old Helmut loves it. Says the fellow plays him all the old Viennese songs. Let's eat.'

He pressed the bell and the old lady came in, bowed to the young man and looked at the Herr Baron.

'Bring it in, Maria. What have we got?'

'Omelette, sir. Mushroom omelettes.'

'Fine, fine. Let's have them.'

When the meal was over the two of them sat in the tapestry chairs, with a decanter of brandy between them.

'How long are you going to be in Berlin, Father?'

'God knows, boy. A month or more from the look of it. We've just been given orders to turn the Brunswick works over to making tank tracks. Three shifts, seven days a week. Each day's production to be despatched the same day to Dortmund and Essen.'

The old man looked with alert eyes at his son.

'You know what this means, Max?'

'Yes. A land war.'

'The Russians?'

'He's always said that that's where the danger lies.'

'I thought when von Ribbentrop signed the pact in Moscow that maybe it would ease the tensions.'

'I think, Father, that that was no more real than the Munich agreement with Chamberlain. But it will be seven or eight months before we could attack the Soviets.'

'Are you sure?'

'By the time the Wehrmacht is regrouped and refitted it will be winter, and then the terrain will be unsuitable for vehicles.'

'When do you think it will be?'

'Next year. Perhaps May, but more likely June.'

71

'Why, oh why, didn't the English accept his peace offer? We shall be back again with our old nightmare – a war on two fronts.'

'They waited for us to invade them. We didn't go. They no longer expect an invasion. I saw an intelligence report that said that Churchill forecast back in May that we should never risk it. But we may prove him wrong yet. There is still time.'

'How long is your leave?'

'Another seven weeks.'

'A long leave for wartime?'

Max von Bayer looked at his father.

'Will you stay in Berlin for the next five or six weeks, Father? I want to use the Schloss to train a few people.'

'I will do as you wish, my boy. It is yours to use,' He smiled. 'Let me know when it's safe for me to come back.'

'I'll play you a game of chess. I'll give you white and a rook's pawn.'

'You know, you were only eleven years old when you first beat me.'

Eight

It took four hours to drive down the autobahn to Brunswick, and another hour and a half before they were at Schloss Eger. Twice they were stopped. Once by the military police and once by a unit of the NSKK. Both times his SS identity card and travel warrants were accepted without question. Kästner had reluctantly agreed to come with him and stay for the initial briefing. Schultz and Kruger slept, unconcerned, in the back of the BMW.

He drove up the long road from the lodge to the main house, and by then everyone was awake. Old Helmut came out for their bags, and von Bayer showed them to their rooms.

They had dinner that evening at the long oak table in the big hall. The servants had laid out crystal and silver and the best starched napery. But there was only potato soup followed by stewed apple. Both from the home farm. There were nods and winks that there would be eggs the next day, and salads.

When the meal was over and he had sent the servants away, von Bayer stood up.

'I want to thank you all for coming here. You know very little about what I intend for us to do. Before I introduce you to each other I want to tell you one piece of background information. I tell you this so that you have an opportunity to change your minds. This will be the *only* opportunity you will have. If you wish to leave I will see that you are taken back to Berlin tonight. If you stay, there will be no second chance. Once you know my plans the team cannot risk any member leaving. So. This is a secret operation. It is not official because the risk of failure is high. But you will be trained, and take orders, as if you were part of the regular armed forces. Is that understood?'

Von Bayer looked round the table. Nobody indicated either agreement or disagreement, except Rudi Kruger who nodded eagerly. Von Bayer went on:

'In a few weeks' time we shall, the six of us, cross the Channel and land in England. We shall destroy aircraft, installations and equipment. We shall return as soon as our mission is completed. *I* shall be in command. My name is Max von Bayer, and I am an officer in the SS with the rank of Sturmbannführer.' He paused. 'I shall tell you no more tonight, my friends. Your room doors are unlocked, you are free to go. If you would be embarrassed to leave in front of the others you can leave during the night. If you wish to leave now, I will provide transport immediately. Thank you.'

There was a creaking of chairs as people relaxed, and then Schultz, who was smoking a cigar, raised his hand.

'You said 'the six of us.' That gentleman . . .' he waved his cigar towards Kästner, '. . . told me he was only an observer. So where are the six?'

'I don't want to introduce you to each other until you have made the decision, but maybe you have not realized that the young lady will be coming with us.'

Schultz smiled his disbelief. 'What's she going to do, for God's sake?'

'Like you, my friend, she's an expert. You'll learn what she will be doing tomorrow.'

Schultz shrugged, and looking round the table for support he smiled at the other men. Only the girl grinned back at him.

Von Bayer stood waiting for further comments and he nodded when Voss put up his hand.

'Do we get paid for this safari?'

'How much do you want, mister?'

Voss smiled. 'I don't need paying, Sturmbannführer. Not for just a few weeks. But others might need it.'

Von Bayer looked around the table. 'Anyone who needs payment should see me privately. Is there anyone who wants transport now?'

Nobody moved or spoke. Von Bayer lifted his glass of wine: *'Hals- und Beinbruch!'*

The response was ragged but audible, and only a smiling Walter Kleist didn't drink his wine.

Von Bayer talked to them for half an hour about his father, and the house, and its outlying land, and then suggested that they all had a good night's rest. They would be called at six the next morning.

Kästner went with von Bayer to his bedroom, sitting on the bed as von Bayer undressed.

'You'll have to watch Schultz. He's got a chip on his shoulder about something. An aggressive bastard. He'll be testing you out, and you'd better put him down first time, or he'll be trouble.'

'I've got plans for Herr Schultz. He won't be a problem.'

Kästner shrugged. 'OK. I'll go back to Berlin tomorrow. Is there anything you want?'

'Yes. A lot.'

'Tell me.'

'I want documents forged. English and our own. Identity cards and special passes for restricted areas.'

Kästner looked at him. 'Even the Abwehr don't get forged documents that easily, Max. It could take weeks.'

'Ten days, Otto. That's all I can spare. There's something else I want too.'

'What's that?'

'The locations of two units near Hanover that have a good sized armoury and an explosives store.'

Kästner stood up. 'I suppose you'll want the *Bismarck* for the Channel crossing. Goodnight, my friend. Don't sit up too late listening for your departing friends. I think somehow they'll all stick with you. You know you reminded me of someone tonight.'

'Who's that?'

'The Pied Piper of Hamelin.'

Von Bayer smiled and slid into his bed. In the brief moments before he slept he wondered what it would feel like to be in the same country as Sadie Aarons.

Otto Schultz looked round his bedroom with mixed feelings. Demolition men are only builders in reverse. You needed to know about building before you could raze brick and concrete structures to the ground. Schloss Eger was well-built by anybody's standards. He estimated that it had been built before Germany became a single entity in 1872. A time when materials and craftsmen were readily available. Even the internal walls were double thickness and the window frames were hand-made and set in good local stone. The door furniture and light fittings were solid brass and even the floors were solid oak. He estimated that it would take a good six months with two teams to get Schloss Eger down to ground level. Longer if he was allowed to dispose of the valuable bits and pieces.

As a demolition expert Otto Schultz found Schloss Eger totally admirable. As a man he found it scandalous. A vulgar, outrageous display of power and money that was typical of the kind of people who put 'von' in front of their names. The finger-snappers with cold grey eyes who complained about taxes but never paid them, who saw men and women as servants and workers, to hire and fire as the mood took them.

Otto Schultz and his brother had been raised, since they were four and three respectively, in an orphanage just outside Berlin. Otto could remember standing in the gloomy entrance hall while his mother signed a paper. And that had been the last they had seen of her. Most of the boys were real orphans, lacking at least one parent but generally both. But the brothers Schultz had a full complement of parents, it was just that they were not wanted. They had survived, as small boys do, but with an aggression and a cynicism that bordered on the pathological. Neither of them had, or desired, any human relationship that was not brief and commercial.

They had both started as labourers on a building site

when they were fourteen. Otto had been the first to leave the orphanage and Fritz had joined him in his dingy room a year later. There was a tolerance but no affection between them and they fended off even the most tentative attempts at friendship from outsiders, be they male or female. They were plain rather than ugly, and as so often happens, their arrogant independence made them attractive to girls. By the time they were sixteen they had both had sexual experience with girls of their own class and by the time they were in their twenties, and financially successful, their conquests came from more exotic areas. There were young women who saw the Schultz brothers as a challenge, wild animals to be tamed, there were others who had visions of marriage and wealth, and the truly innocent who misread their animal lust as a sign of affection or love. The only survivors were those who merely enjoyed the animal lust. Not even the shrewder girls recognized the urgent copulation as a kind of revenge on the mother who gave them away. In Fritz's case the revenge was probably subconscious. In Otto's case it was deliberate and calculated, and part of the pleasure.

The Schultz brothers, on a more mundane level, knew how to run a very successful business. Fritz knew how to use money and how to avoid paying taxes. They had twenty-two bank accounts between them and under the shack in the yard were four large metal boxes buried four feet down. And as befitted their owners' speciality, the hole was properly lined with oak planking carefully braced. Inside the boxes were jewellery, gold coins and uncut diamonds bought from Polish refugees.

Otto Schultz undressed slowly, folding his clothes neatly and carefully, placing them on the tapestry chair. As he pulled the blankets over his shoulders he thought briefly of the girl. She was one of those cool society lovelies who looked like they didn't know what it was all about. The kind who just lay there and let you do it to them. She seemed to be attached to the Kleist fellow but he looked like a homo with those big sad brown eyes and the wavy hair. He turned on to his side and was asleep almost instantly.

Walter Kleist lay on his back on the double bed, his dark skin emphasized by the clean white sheets. Ushi Lange had slipped a copy of *Die Welt* under his body to avoid staining the bed linen. Kleist was naked, and across his flat stomach was a huge area of livid flesh. Smooth and featureless except for the ridge of muscle that gleamed wetly from the suppurating surface of the burns. Slowly and carefully the girl's hand smoothed the oil over the raw flesh as Kleist lay with the fingers of his right hand between his teeth to stop him from crying out. The raw red wound wandered from his belly to cascade over his hip and across the muscles at the front of his thigh.

Kruger and Voss in their separate quarters had both said their prayers, Kruger kneeling beside his bed and Voss under the comfort of the blankets. It took Kruger some time to overcome his excitement at being chosen for such a venture, but Voss read for only a few minutes before he switched off the light and slept.

Nine

Von Bayer had been shaken awake by old Helmut just before five o'clock and he was sipping the hot chocolate before he remembered where he was and what he was doing. For a moment it seemed like some crazy mixed-up dream, and then, just as quickly, his thoughts were back under control.

Nobody had left during the night but von Bayer sensed a feeling of anti-climax from the group. By seven o'clock everybody had eaten, and he invited them into one of the smaller reception rooms in the wing of the house. He had already prepared it for the meeting. There were two trestle tables, and a chair for each person. There was a large map on the wall that showed the coast and hinterland on both sides of the Channel.

He had introduced each of them with brief details of their backgrounds and their function in the operation. For an hour he had told them of the plans for Sea-Lion without any criticism of any of the armed services. Then he gave them an outline of his own plans. When that was done he turned to Schultz.

'Otto, I want you to give an informal talk on explosives and demolition. I want everybody to be capable of at least carrying out a simple demolition sabotage operation after Otto gives the details of what has to be done. You've got fourteen days to learn each other's skills.' He turned to point at Kruger. 'Rudi, I want you to act as back-up for Fräulein Lange.' He turned to Voss. 'Erich, I want you to give an hour's weapons instruction every day, and in a few days' time we shall be in a position to have a practice shoot every day. This evening I'll show you the handbooks that were prepared for Sea-Lion and tell you something of conditions in England at the moment. So you take over first, Otto.'

He walked with Kästner to his father's study and drew up two chairs for them.

'Can I go through the list of documents that I need, Otto?'

Kästner smiled wryly. 'By all means. But don't take it for granted that I can get them.'

'I want a first-class British civilian identity card for each one of us. I want British medical certificates and service papers that class us as unfit for military service or honourably discharged on medical grounds. And I want three thousand English pounds – genuine. I'll give you a cheque for the Reichsmark equivalent. And I want the name and present location of that U-boat lieutenant who was seconded to the planning group from Admiral Saalwächter's HQ in Paris. The cheeky one.'

Kästner sighed. 'What names do you want on the documents?'

'You decide, Otto, but keep the same initials. And forenames the same if there is an English equivalent.'

'The U-Boat lieutenant is a Karl Westphal and he's at the U-Boat pens at Brest.'

'Have our Sea-Lion passes been withdrawn or cancelled?'

'Not so far as I know. It could happen any day.'

'You look full of doubts, Otto. Are you?'

Kästner looked past von Bayer to where he could see the lawns sweeping up to the edge of the woods. There were sheep and fat lambs grazing at the edge of the lawns. Then for a few moments he closed his eyes. Von Bayer waited in silence. It was several minutes before Kästner spoke.

'When I listened to you talking to the others just now, I realized how different we are, you and I. I spend my time reading reports, analysing situations, forecasting what might happen next. Suggesting possible operations and helping to organize them. Other people do the dirty work. I've never done an act of violence in my life. I've never killed a man or even injured a man. I can't imagine ever doing such a thing. But you're a doer. A man of action. Sure of yourself and sure that others will follow just because you say they should. You've got courage. Moral courage and physical courage. And I have wisdom and experience.'

'That makes a good combination, Otto.'

Kästner sighed deeply. 'I know, Max. I know. But in my wisdom or my ignorance I look at that bunch of invalids and I don't see a winning team. If you had half a dozen para-troopers or panzermen I could just about believe. With these people I can't make up my mind whether you are brave or just foolish.' Slowly he opened his eyes and looked at von Bayer. 'Have you really thought it through, Max?'

Von Bayer spoke quietly. 'You saw what happened, Otto, with Sea-Lion, when people want every aspect perfectly planned. You end up doing nothing. Even with my invalids I can succeed. And they aren't all invalids. Only Walter Kleist is really an invalid.'

'And Kruger with only one lung that really works.'

'OK. Two invalids but they're volunteers. They both know their stuff.'

Kästner stood up. 'I'll come back in three or four days, Max. If I'm very lucky I'll have what you want. Then I'll stay with you until you go. Maybe I can help.'

'Thanks, Otto.'

Von Bayer walked slowly back to the room where he had left the others. They barely looked up as he went into the room and stood silently leaning against the door. Schultz was standing, leaning over the table pointing at a sheet of paper. He nodded to the girl.

'Show me where you put the charge.'

She pointed to a spot on the paper.

'Not bad. Now you.' And he nodded at Voss who said, 'At the corner.'

'Why?'

'Then it brings down both walls.'

Schultz nodded and looked around the group.

'Any other comments?'

They were all silent.

'Well, you would have done a fair amount of damage but remember what I said about secondary blast. One light charge then a second major charge, and you get a geared effect of a big bang on a weakened structure.'

Schultz turned, hesitating, towards von Bayer.

'Do you want to take over, Herr Sturmbannführer?'

Von Bayer nodded but didn't move from the door.

'Herr Voss, I'd like you to take everybody outside when you've covered the weapons. Anywhere you like so long as it is inside the estate. Take the maps of the area from the small table in the corner. Start teaching them map reading and a bit of fieldcraft. This afternoon I want to talk to you about the area we shall be operating in. This evening we shall have a general discussion. Then we'll eat and if we are all very good Herr Kleist might play for us. Lunch is at one o'clock. Bread and an apple. We'll have our eggs tonight. Herr Voss.'

Voss stood up slowly, smoothing his moustache as he looked around the table. Then from his pocket he took a Luger and laid it on the table.

'A Luger pistol, ladies and gentlemen. Designed by the son of a dentist, from the original by Borchard. The magazine holds eight shots and I'm going to teach you how to fire it and strip it. The Wehrmacht take six weeks to teach their recruits, I hope to do it in four days. We've got rifles and sub-machine-guns to cover as well.' He lifted the gun and with finger and thumb pulled out the magazine. 'The rounds are 9 mm parabellum. Let me explain why we . . .'

Von Bayer quietly opened the door and left. They were fantastic he thought, and his vague depression lifted as he walked back to his father's study.

It was early evening when Voss knocked on the study door and waited. He knocked again, and von Bayer called out to him to come in.

'Apologies, Herr Sturmbannführer, may I have a word with you?'

'Take a seat, Erich. What's the problem?'

'It's Walter Kleist. He's a very courageous man but he should not be doing fieldwork. In fact I think he should be in hospital.'

'What makes you think that?'

'It's not just me. We all think the same.' The blue eyes looked at him intently. 'Have you seen his body?'

'No. I haven't.

'Schultz heard him scream and went to find him. He had been caught in a thorn-bush. Schultz had to tear away his shirt to get him free and our Walter fainted. Schultz came to fetch me over. Herr Sturmbannführer, that man's body is like an open wound. He must be in permanent pain.'

'What are you suggesting?'

'We shouldn't take him. It's not fair to him or to the rest of us. A sick man in enemy territory would be a great burden.'

'He hasn't got long to live, Erich. He knows that. To leave him behind would be another wound. And the girl would not come without him.'

'And if he is mortally ill while we are on our mission, what then?'

'He would have to surrender himself.'

'And give us all away.'

'He wouldn't do that, Erich. No more than you and I would.'

'Under torture.'

'The British wouldn't torture a dying man. No more than we should.'

'There are always men, my friend, who will find a war an excuse for behaving like animals.'

'I'll think about it, Erich. Thanks for letting me know. But I agree. No more fieldwork for Walter.'

After Voss had gone von Bayer sat at his father's desk thinking. Already Kleist was 'our Walter'. It was a good sign. And then there was a peremptory knock on the door. Schultz came in.

'You busy, friend?'

'Come in, Otto. Sit down.'

Schultz was smoking a cigar and his sleeves, as always, were rolled up to the elbow.

'Did old man Voss talk to you about Kleist?'

'Yes.'

'We can't take him, that's for sure. He's a liability.'

'Why?'

'Have you seen his body? It's like raw meat. How'd he get that anyway? It looks like a burn to me.'

'He was an officer in a Panzer kommando in Poland. That's what a flame-thrower does. He got the Knight's Cross for that.'

Schultz drew on his cigar and slowly blew out the smoke. Then he stood up and walked to the window and stood looking out. It seemed a long time before he turned and looked at von Bayer.

'Why do you want him. What's he gonna do?'

'I wanted one other person who had had army training. He's got a good record, and he's got guts. And he volunteered.'

Schultz looked at von Bayer's face. 'Why didn't they give you soldiers to do this job?'

'It isn't an official operation, Otto. It's off the record. If we succeed then we get our medals. If we fail, nobody will ever hear about us.'

'You want to take Kleist?'

'I do. And he wants to go.'

Schultz nodded slowly. 'I'll look after Walter Kleist. Leave him to me.'

'I wanted to talk to you anyway, Otto.'

'What about?'

'I want you to be second-in-command.'

The surprise on Schultz's face was genuine.

'Christ, I'm not a bloody soldier. Why me?'

'You will be in three weeks' time, Otto. But if you're scared . . .'

Schultz's thick, calloused forefinger wagged angrily, and his face was flushed with anger.

'Don't you ever . . .' Then he saw the smile on von Bayer's face and he said quietly. 'Von Bayer, you are a cunning bastard.' He paused and then said, 'Yes. I'll be your second-in-command.'

'Let's go and eat, Otto. And "old" Voss is forty-five.'
'That's old enough,' Schultz said.

Von Bayer had gone up to Kleist's room and knocked. The girl had opened the door with her finger to her lips.

'How is he?' von Bayer whispered.

She walked out into the corridor quietly closing the door behind her.

'He's slept for an hour. He'll be fine when he wakes up.'

'I hear that he got hurt badly.'

She sighed. 'Not by his standards, Max. It caught him napping. It was just a different kind of pain. But he's worried that the others won't want him now they've seen his burns.'

'Otto Schultz has appointed himself Walter's guardian.'

'I can't understand that man. He's so arrogant. So crude.'

Von Bayer nodded. 'He'll look after Walter, Ushi. D'you think Walter would be fit enough to come down in half an hour and play to us?'

'I should think so. Providing he wakes up.'

'Would you sing as well?'

She smiled. 'Yes. I'll sing you "*Ich schenk' mein Herz*".'

There had been an egg for each of them and wild blackberries and a bowl of cream. Nobody talked much and von Bayer knew that the incident with Kleist had affected them all. They were torn between sympathy for the man himself and awareness that he could be a weak link in the chain.

Von Bayer had told Helmut to light a log fire in the main living-room and there was a half bottle of brandy and glasses on the low table.

It was Otto Schultz who first noticed Kleist and the girl coming down the wide staircase. He pushed back his chair, stood up and walked over to the foot of the stairs. As Kleist got to the bottom he was smiling. But there were beads of perspiration standing out on his face.

Von Bayer walked out over to join them.

'How are you feeling, Walter?'

'Fine, my boy. It's just old age. You want me to play you a tune or two, yes?'

85

'If you feel like it.'

'Lead on. Are you going to let old Helmut join us. He's rather fond of my kind of *schmaltz*.'

'He's pouring out coffee for us now.'

Kleist made himself comfortable at the piano and the girl leaned with her arms folded on the top and watched Kleist's face as he started to play. He half-turned on the piano stool.

'The first five numbers are for *den alten Helmut*.'

For the next ten minutes Kleist played Strauss waltzes with a gusto and energy that belied his pain. He ended with the waltz from *Der Rosenkavalier* and there was a second's silence when he finished before they applauded.

Then there were all the well-loved songs from the Viennese operettas. Ushi Lange sang *'Ich schenk' mein Herz'* and finally, very softly, *'Sag' beim Abschied'*. The applause was enthusiastic and she was amused when von Bayer asked her to sing his song one last time.

When, finally, Kleist closed the piano and turned round to face the others, von Bayer stood up and thanked them both and then turned to the others.

'And now, gentlemen, we come back to earth. Tonight we become soldiers. We don't go to bed. Tonight we do our first night-work. Herr Voss will show you on a map how you get to the woods on the estate called Kleiner Mittelwald. Inside that wood is a hunting lodge. I want you to go out one at a time. You'll be given ninety minutes each to come back with your own sketch of the woods and your recommended route to get to the lodge. So, Herr Voss, will you put this in hand. Walter and Ushi, you both stay behind. Walter will check your maps and debrief you, and Ushi will keep the coffee-pot going for your return.' He nodded towards Voss but before he could speak old Helmut came back in the room.

'Freiherr von Bayer. A telephone call for you from Berlin.'

Von Bayer nodded. 'Carry on, Herr Voss.'

It was Kästner on the telephone and he sounded tired.

'Are you alone, Max?'

'More or less.'

'D'you want a short-wave radio?'

'What model?'

86

'Siemens 127.'

'Let me speak to Ushi. Hang on.'

A few minutes later he was back.

'The answer is "yes" if we can have two spare crystals.'

'That's no problem. I'll be back the day after tomorrow. Your luck still seems to be holding.'

'Are you coming back by car?'

'Providing I can get petrol. Why?'

'I'll call you tomorrow. Will you be around?'

'Not until the evening.'

'I'll call you about six.'

'How are the merry men?'

'Fine.'

Kästner laughed and hung up.

It was dawn before von Bayer went to bed.

Ten

In London, the Lord Mayor had started a fund for the relief of the distress caused by the bombing. The Lord Mayor of Melbourne and the American Ambassador had launched similar funds. But on some nights there were ugly scenes outside the closed Tube stations when crowds sought them out for shelter. Churchill overruled his advisers and ordered them to be opened.

The warships *Nelson* and *Hood* had moved down from Rosyth and hundreds of men were busy repairing Fighter Command's airfields and installations before the next onslaught of the Luftwaffe. The German bomber formations were being broken up over Canterbury and Maidstone but enough got through to cause damage and casualties in London.

On the last day of September 1940, Neville Chamberlain told the Prime Minister that he was dying of cancer and could no longer stay as a member of the War Cabinet. The *Sunday Pictorial* and the *Daily Mirror* printed slashing articles on the Government, and Churchill saw them as a sinister move to prepare the country for a surrender peace. The whole country, from its leaders to the bombed-out East Enders, held its breath as it waited for the invaders. Twice the codeword 'Cromwell' had been issued, to warn of immediate invasion. Once in error, but once by the Chiefs of Staff. And mistakenly, church bells had been rung in Kent and Sussex thinking that the invasion had actually started. Every night the German bombers circled a London that seemed almost defenceless. Even the shelterers in the Tube stations were being killed, and there were nights when a thousand fires overwhelmed the fire service. And by 1 October only Paddington and King's Cross stations were still in use. The Luftwaffe's bombers were still attacking the south-coast ports by day and night and it was assumed that their raids were still a preliminary to invasion.

Uneasy reports were filtering back to the War Cabinet from Madrid that the Germans were planning an attack on Greece and Yugoslavia. It was becoming obvious that the Wehrmacht could launch attacks in any direction they chose, and on as many fronts as they chose.

While the War Cabinet and the Chiefs of Staff dealt with that day's problems and the problems to come, with no possi-bility of counter-attack on any front, and defence their only option, the public made up its own mind. It was as if the man in the street knew something that his leaders didn't know. The public had decided that whatever was going to happen, the invasion was no longer imminent. God or the Fates had decided that they would live to fight another day. The night skies over the cities might be red with fires but that was something they were coping with. While the War Cabinet wrestled with agenda that raised problems across the whole of the Empire, the home public settled back for a long war. Not for them the intelligence reports that indicated that Spain was on the verge of enter-ing the war on the Axis side or that the Vichy French were being offered participation in the New Order if they offered French troops to fight against the British in North Africa. Every day, every hour, brought new problems and new pres-sures. The reports that came in from British ambassadors all round the world brought news and rumours of German ac-tivities from Norway to Egypt, from Washington to Tokyo. Churchill marvelled at the public's confidence, and was glad that it was unaware of the disasters inevitably ahead; every-where he went he was welcomed and applauded.

Moshe and Rachael Aarons sat in the front row trying to genuinely admire the display of hydrangeas and geraniums that spread across the base of the platform. But Moshe's mind was on his father. How proud he would have been to be here tonight. He had accepted philosophically that his son had no interest in music. His granddaughter would have been a happy substitute.

The hall was full. A fair number of soldiers and airmen behind the local worthies in the first two rows. Moshe Aarons was an emotional man and he wished that they would lower the lights so that he could brush the tears from his eyes. He couldn't have given a reason for his tears. It certainly wasn't sadness. Maybe it was because this was a culmination of too many things. He had tried to absorb the words of praise about his daughter but he couldn't. The praise itself was enough. The reasons didn't matter. They prophesied a brilliant career. Not a prodigy, she was too old for that. She had a career and they said she would undoubtedly be successful and that was enough for Moshe Aarons.

He had spent ninety pounds on the new 'cello. It wasn't an Amati but it was 'school of Amati' and that dark-brown figure-of-eight instrument was the love of her life. And this was her first professional engagement. Ten guineas. And she was still at music school. It would have been better still if David could have been there. But the Army had sent him to some godforsaken place in Scotland to interrogate German agents who landed in rubber dinghies from the submarines that lay off the coast. They came with a regular time-table and were no trouble to anybody. Men who had worked as waiters or salesmen in England. Sent like lambs to the slaughter.

The orchestra was settling into its seats and the oboe was giving them an 'A'. The first item was to be the Beethoven Overture *Leonora* No. 3. There had been much public debate about playing Teutonic music but tolerance had prevailed.

There was loud applause for the conductor who bowed only briefly to the audience and turned back to his musicians. He tried to care as he listened but his mind was on his daughter. He said a small prayer for her and then one for himself for being outside his home on a Friday evening. And suddenly they were applauding and a smiling girl was lifting her 'cello high as she weaved her way through the orchestra to the gilt chair at the front of the stage to the conductor's left. And Moshe Aarons felt a glow of affection for the conductor who was so obviously concerned to put the young girl at her ease. Then a smile and an exchange of nods and they were off. It was the Elgar 'Cello Concerto and Moshe Aarons had a shrewd suspicion as to why she had chosen that particular work.

He watched and listened intently, slightly in awe of the concentration on his daughter's face and her self-assurance as she bent over the instrument, sweeping back her long black hair when she wasn't playing. This was *his* daughter, and he wanted to go out in the street and tell people, fetch them in from the highways and byways to witness the miracle. This was once that fat solemn-faced baby that slept in the old-fashioned wooden cot at the foot of his bed. Sadie Aarons, concert 'cellist.

The applause was enthusiastic but Moshe Aarons clapped very modestly. When the concert was over he walked with his wife to the greenroom. It was crowded with friends of the performers. They had had only a few brief moments with Sadie, a peck on the cheek, admiration for three bouquets and the news that Colin would bring her home. Late. He wasn't to wait up.

But he did wait up, with the glass of milk and the two biscuits on the silver salver and the whisky for himself. It was almost two o'clock when he heard her let herself in. She came into the room, her face glowing and rain on her cheeks looking like an advertisement for Ovaltine. She propped her 'cello in its canvas case against the piano and came over and kissed him. She took the glass of milk and sat down opposite him on the settee.

'Did you like the concert, O Philistine?'

He smiled. 'I liked the middle bit. She was very pretty.'

'You're incorrigible, Daddy.'

'How was Colin?'

'Fine, as usual. A bit emotional but that was probably the

Elgar.' She leaned forward and put her glass on the coffee table. 'He asked me to marry him again.'

'When did he ask you before?'

'It's a monthly event actually.'

'And what did you say?'

'No. As usual.'

'And was that the Elgar too?'

He cursed himself for saying it but the compulsion had been too great.

The beautiful brown eyes looked across at him. She said softly, 'What made you say that?'

'I'm a fool, that's why.'

'You're not. Whatever you are, you're not that.'

'OK. I withdraw the question. And it's time we were both in bed.'

But the brown eyes still gazed at him. 'You remembered, didn't you?'

'Of course I did. I love you and you were desperately unhappy, and there was nothing I could do to help.'

'You did what you thought was right to protect me.'

'What should I have done, my love?'

She sighed deeply and then looked up at him. 'I think you did what you should have done. But I won't ever stop loving him.'

'Did you love him at that time?'

'I know now that I did. But at the time I was too young and too stupid.'

'Have you ever loved anyone else?'

'No. Never. And I never will. I'll wait for him.'

'He may be married, sweetheart.'

'He isn't.'

'How do you know?'

'I just know.'

And he saw two fat tears run down her cheeks. He reached out and took her hand.

'Is there anything I could do, we could do, to help.'

She gulped. 'Yes. Just talk about him sometimes. Don't pretend he never happened.'

'Tell me what you liked about him.'

She smiled through the tears. 'He was handsome, he was gentle, he loved me and he never made a pass at me or tried to take advantage of my naïveté.'

He smiled. 'That's a pretty good list, sweetie. I'll remember that. Have you got a photograph of him?'

She nodded. 'Yes. I got one from the local paper.'

'Let's frame it and put it on top of the piano. The place of honour.'

She put her head in her hands and sobbed and all he could do was curse himself and stroke that slender, vulnerable young neck.

By the end of the second week in October von Bayer knew that his five recruits were now a team. They had trained for long hours without complaint and had carried out minor enterprises with confidence. Schultz and Kruger had gone back to Berlin and gathered together explosives and detonators from Schultz's yard, and plastic explosive from an unguarded Abwehr store marked down by Kästner. Voss had trained them to handle all the weapons at their disposal and Ushi Lange had mastered the Wehrmacht radio in half a day.

They had been paired off; Kruger and the girl, Voss and Kleist, and Schultz with von Bayer. Von Bayer knew that they were all overconfident, they were beginning to celebrate as if the training was itself the operation. Each night Kleist played and the girl sang, and by now von Bayer's favourite song was like some talisman, Kruger whistled it while he helped Voss stripping and oiling the weapons, and even Schultz had been seen to sway in time to the music. They were seldom asleep before the early hours of the morning but they were fitter than they had been when they first came to Schloss Eger.

Kästner had brought back the documentation they needed and the English speakers, Voss, Kleist, the girl, and von Bayer had listened every evening to the news bulletins from the BBC, and every day von Bayer went over the Sea-Lion material that showed aerial photographs of towns and villages up to thirty miles back from the coast of Kent and Sussex. Their clothes had been stripped of all labels and markings that would identify them as German and they had been given their identity cards, passes and ration cards and clothing coupons. In each bedroom the things they would be allowed to take were kept separate from the rest of their personal belongings, and in his father's study von Bayer had typed lists of everything that would go with them.

Von Bayer was soaked to the skin but he kept the chestnut to a walk. Kästner would not be back for at least two hours and he needed to make the time go by until he heard his news. On the telephone he had sounded non-committal and when he had tried to probe some indication from him Kästner had hung up. The line from Brest was heavy with static and it had been impossible to gauge anything from Kästner's voice. He had been away for five days now and that could mean that he had had difficulties, or it could mean that he was actually discussing the details. Kästner had told him before he had left to expect a completely negative response, and, as if that were not enough, he had said that he was already uneasy that everything had so far gone so smoothly. He consoled himself that Kästner had never had military experience. He was a staff man not a field man. And von Bayer knew from his SS training that boldness always paid off. He had bluffed his way into top security installations in the training exercises because he believed his own bluff. Only once had he been caught and that was when the instructors had given the cold-bath treatment to one of his squad and had got all the details of his plan. They were teaching him a lesson and he had learned the lesson. Nobody on his team, apart from Kästner, knew where he was aiming to land or what his targets would be.

The rain had stopped, there was a patch of blue in the sky, and a heat mist was rising already from the side of the hill. It would be a fine evening and they could do a night walk to check their compass reading. Only Voss and Kleist were able to navigate by the stars and Voss still looked sometimes for the Southern Cross before he remembered where he was. If they had to hang around too long their elation could easily exaggerate into euphoria or deteriorate into apprehension. He wanted them on an even keel, because he knew that their present easy co-operation and comradeship could disappear as soon as they were under real pressure. It was only competence and self-confidence that kept a group together under active service conditions.

At the stables he waved the lad away, unbuckled the girth and heaved off the saddle. He led the horse to its stall and placed the saddle on its post. Slowly and carefully he wiped down the chestnut and groomed it until its coat shone and its hooves were black with oil. He tried to push all thoughts of the operation from his mind. When he was on his own, without the stimulus of organization, his thoughts swung too often to extremes that saw the operation as either entirely routine and normal or an act of madness doomed to disaster. He knew that he must get his team across the Channel as soon as possible.

Kästner was back by nine o'clock, and went straight to von Bayer's room. Von Bayer was listening to the BBC news and he switched the radio off immediately. Kästner's face looked haggard and pale, his eyes red-rimmed.

'Is it bad news, Otto?'

Kästner sighed deeply and closed his eyes. 'No. It could be good news. Leutnant Westphal is outside in the car. But he needs to leave almost immediately. You've got half an hour to convince him that it's not some trick to implicate him as a traitor.'

'We wouldn't be landing in enemy territory if we were traitors.'

'Why not? You could be escaping, not fighting.'

'My God, I never thought of that. What have you told him?'

'Everything. He's sympathetic. He remembers you. It fits in with his sailing orders. But he needs convincing.'

'Shall I go out to the car?'

'You'd better. He refuses to come in.'

Von Bayer slipped his arms into his jacket and walked with Kästner to where the car was parked without lights in the curve of the drive. The naval officer was sitting in the back and von Bayer slid in beside him as Kästner got into the front. Von Bayer held out his hand and with only slight hesitation the naval officer took it.

'Herr Leutnant. Many thanks for making this journey. Tell me how I can persuade you to help me?'

'How many of you are there?'

'Six including me. Five men, one girl. She's the radio operator.'

'And how many of you are deserters?'

'None.'

'I thought you were an SS officer.'

'I am. But I'm not deserting. The others are all civilians and one has an honourable discharge from the Wehrmacht and a Knight's Cross.'

'How do I know that you are not deserting?'

'I am officially on leave. I have more than three weeks' leave still to go. I hope to be back in that time.'

Westphal said quietly, 'And how do you intend to get back?'

'I've no idea. I shall be liaising by radio with Kästner. I hope he can arrange for us to be picked up officially.'

'Have you discussed with Kästner any plan for your return?'

'No.'

'Has he?' Westphal looked at Kästner.

'Not yet.'

'Do you believe his story about what he is going to do?'

'Yes. I've helped him recruit the others.'

Westphal turned to look at von Bayer. 'Tell me one of the targets you intend attacking.'

'The high-level radar station at Lympne.'

'What does it look like?'

'I've got photographs. It's four tall pylons, you can see it from ten miles off the coast.'

'Where do you want to land?'

'About four miles east of Camber. Along the coast from Rye.'

Westphal sat silently and then he turned to Kästner.

'Your identity card says that you are a colonel in the Abwehr, yes?'

'Yes. I am.'

'Will you sign a statement that I dictate taking full responsibility that these people are engaged in a clandestine attack on the enemy?'

'I will not sign any statement that they are official.'

'I didn't ask for that.'

'Then I'll sign. D'you want to check with Berlin that I am an Abwehr officer?'

'I did that after our first talk, Herr Oberst.'

Westphal looked back at von Bayer.

'Have you got charts of the coast at Camber?'

'Yes. I've got the Sea-Lion charts.'

'Where are they?'

'In the house.'

'I'd better come in with you.'

The three of them sat at the desk in the study with the charts in front of them. Alongside the chart was the Sea-Lion handbook that showed photographs and sketches of the whole of the Kent and Sussex coasts. There were sketches made by German tourists, reproductions from local newspapers, tourist postcards of seaside towns, and photographs taken from German merchant-ships and U-boats.

Leutnant Westphal looked silently at the charts, then he looked up at von Bayer.

'I'm due to take my boat to sea on the 21st or 22nd. My orders will be to join other U-boats in the North Sea to try out new tactics against the convoys leaving from Methil in Scotland. I would be prepared to lie off the coast and land you by dinghy. I'll navigate to Rye and then it will depend on the mine-field reports as to how near I can drop you to Camber. Have any of you ever been on a U-boat?'

'I haven't. I'm sure the others haven't either.'

'It's going to be a very uncomfortable journey. You'll be sleeping on armed torpedoes for at least two days. You'll be exhausted by the time you get there.'

'That doesn't matter.'

'How much equipment have you got?'

'It's nearly a thousand kilos.'

'Bulky?'

'No.'

'Make out an emergency list of stuff you can abandon if necessary. Up to two hundred kilos.'

'It's an absolute minimum already, Herr Leutnant.'

'That's up to you. Those are my orders.'

'What kind of dinghy will it be?'

'A *schlauchboot* – an inflated rubber dinghy. You'll have to destroy it or it will give your position away. You can't burn it, it would smoke like hell. You'll have to cut it up and bury it.'

'When do you want us at Brest?'

'I'll give you thirty-six hours' notice. You'll report straight to me at U-boat 210.'

'Can you give us passes to the docks?'

'Yes. You'll have to send someone back with me.' He turned to look at Kästner. 'Can you come back with me?'

'How about a night's sleep?'

'Sure. You can sleep in the car. I'll drive.'

'Why don't you stop and have a meal with us and meet the others.'

Westphal looked at Kästner who nodded.

'An hour then. No longer.'

Like most Germans old Helmut held the Kriegsmarine and its officers in the highest esteem, an esteem that was only just short of worship. With a U-boat commander in uniform in the house the evening meal had to be something special. The stable-boy was sent off with a torch to check the snares at the edge of the woods and the fine onion soup had been followed by rabbit. And there was cream and raisins with the baked apples. And Leutnant Westphal had sung a duet with Ushi Lange. He had a good tenor voice and they had had to sing '*Wien, Wien nur du allein*' twice before he was allowed to take his tot of brandy. It was well after midnight when he and Kästner finally left for the long journey back to Brest.

With only five days to go von Bayer concentrated on training them on the approach through the woods to the hunting lodge. Time and again he had sat in the lodge listening for the tell-tale silence of the birds or the snapping of a twig as Voss brought them through the undergrowth. There were times now when they could all get within two metres of the lodge without being spotted, and at night they could do it every time.

Kästner had brought back the passes signed by Westphal that would get them inside the security zone and to the submarine pens. They were classified as civilian artificers and armourers.

It was on the fourth day that the call came through from Westphal. They were to report to him by 18:00 hours on the 22nd. This gave them two days and two nights for the journey provided they set off by midnight that same night. Von Bayer had planned a more formal start to their journey but after they had loaded the two cars and the van he told them to rest until they were called. When he roused them all at midnight there was a moment's panic when he found Schultz's room empty and the bed not slept in. It had taken ten minutes' searching before they discovered that he was already in his seat in the car. Asleep.

Kästner had walked with von Bayer to the Mercedes. Kästner held out his hand. 'Radio on net every hour from nine until midnight, your local time. No code. In clear, but brief. Best of luck.' He put a hand on von Bayer's shoulder. '*Hals- und Beinbruch!*'

'*Hals- und Beinbruch!*'

Von Bayer drove the Mercedes, the van came next, driven by Kruger, and Kleist brought up the rear in the BMW.

They were not stopped until the frontier at Aachen and von Bayer's Sea-Lion pass and the pass for Brest were accepted without question. Von Bayer was in uniform and neither the civil police nor the field police were anxious to fall foul of SS Sturmbannführers.

They had rested for an hour at the edge of the forest outside Cambrai and by the evening they were at Louviers, just south of Rouen. They had eaten there and rested for an hour and changed drivers. They had been stopped by a

Wehrmacht patrol a few kilometres outside Rennes but although their documents had been gone over carefully they had been passed through the check-point.

At Morlaix von Bayer had telephoned Westphal who agreed to meet them at the dock gates. There had been two checks before they were at the docks and even with Westphal escorting them there were two more spot checks by security police. But the documents were genuine, and nobody outside the planning group knew for certain that Sea-Lion was not still operational.

Westphal's crewmen had loaded their stores while Westphal himself took them to the dock-side canteen. The coffee was real, not *ersatz*, and the eggs were fresh. The Kriegsmarine did itself well.

As they walked back to the boat Westphal stopped and gathered them around him.

'My men know that you're not sailors. They know that what you're doing is secret and dangerous. You will not talk in front of my men about what you are about to do. Not a word. Is that understood?'

They nodded, and he went on. 'When we release you men in the dinghy we shall back off and submerge. And at that point you'll be on your own. And there'll be no turning back. We shall not be there. If they've seen you we shall not help you, we've got problems enough of our own. If you want something to remember just look over my shoulder. The battleship you can see there is the *Gneisenau*. At the end of World War One when the German fleet surrenderd in the Firth of Forth, the British Admiral Beatty gave an order – he said, "The German ensign will be lowered at sunset and will not be hoisted again". The *Gneisenau* is part of our answer to Admiral Beatty. And maybe you are part of our answer too. My crew and I wish you the best of luck and we'll be thinking of you when we are heading north.'

And formally and stiffly he shook each of their hands.

They had been shown to their quarters and blankets had been laid out for them in the spaces between the torpedoes.

There was only the dimmest light from the bulkhead fittings, and the air was hot and overlaid with the smell of hot oil and chlorine. The sides of their enclosure were a maze of pipes and valves. A continuous clanging came from the hull as the ship was prepared for sailing. Instinctively they talked in whispers.

An hour later the air seemed even warmer and they could hear the chattering of the Enigma coding machine from the control room, and then the whole structure shuddered as the U-boat moved out of the pen. They could hear shouted orders and responses, but they couldn't hear the words. Two hours later Westphal came back to look at them. Only Kleist and the girl were awake. Westphal said, 'Tell von Bayer that we are on the surface now and we shall be there for another three hours. Then we shall dive. It's best if you are all awake when that happens. You'll hear the klaxon, but don't worry, it won't be an emergency. It sounds pretty frightening the first time you hear it but it's just a routine signal. One of my boys will bring you a hot drink and biscuits when we're down to operational level.'

'How long before we get to our RV?'

'It depends on what's happening up above and what information we get from Naval Group West. They are our contact until we get well into the Channel. There could be new mine-fields, or enemy patrols on the surface. Anyway, don't worry. Everything's under control.'

He smiled and left them.

Only Schultz was still asleep when the klaxons went, and minutes later they felt the tilting of the submarine. There was no echo now from the noises of metal on metal, and the voices of the crew seemed muffled as the boat sank lower and lower. Although the dive was slow and gradual, when the axis of the submarine levelled out they felt disorientated. Schultz stood up, and stretching his arms fell sprawling across one of the torpedoes because his sense of balance was still not functioning correctly. It seemed a long time before the coffee came.

There was very little talking and it was not long before they were all sleeping, their bodies moving restlessly in the cramped, unyielding space between the torpedoes.

They had been at sea ten hours by the next time Westphal came forward to see them. He looked across to von Bayer.

'If we have any choice, what time would you prefer to land. Before midnight or after?'

'How long will it take us from the boat to the shore?'

'You'll be on a flood tide. Twenty minutes, give or take five minutes.'

'I'd like to touch land at roughly one o'clock.'

'We're making better time than I expected but there's a British convoy about ten miles ahead of us, and they're being attacked at the moment by fighter-bombers from Calais. If they scatter that could hold us up.'

'Aren't they a target for you?'

'No. Our orders are to join the others in the North Sea. It's to be a trial of a new system called "wolf-packs" with four or five U-boats attacking a convoy together. Something that Kretschmer has worked out. Right. I'll send you down more coffee and a sandwich. The toilets are portside.' He thumped the side of the hull in confirmation.

Von Bayer sat uncomfortably with his head against a bulkhead, recalling yet again the route from the beach to the Military Canal and then across to the farmhouse that had been left empty since it had had its back blown off in a Luftwaffe raid. It was only a mile from the farm where the 9th Army would have made its first-day HQ.

Von Bayer came to suddenly. A rating was bent over him patting his cheek. 'The Commander's compliments, sir. He wants you to come amidships.' Von Bayer struggled awkwardly to his feet and stepped over sleeping bodies until he was clear of the torpedoes. At the bulkhead he stopped and leaned against it, supported by his arms as a wave of nausea swept over him. The rating waited patiently and a few moments later they walked on through a small galley and past a set of bunks.

Leutnant Westphal, with his knees bent, was looking

through the periscope, turning it in a wide arc. After a few moments he stood up.

'Take a quick look. Hastings is due north and we are lying off nearly four miles.'

Von Bayer bent down and fitted his eyes to the double eye-piece. At first he could see nothing, the whole screen seemed to be solid black; then as his eyes adjusted he saw moonlight reflected from a barrage balloon and a pale grey line that could have been the silhouette of a sprawl of buildings. Then Westphal spoke.

'Turn slowly to 230 on the graticule. Slowly. Look for a faint line of white. That's the bar at the entrance to Rye Harbour.' Von Bayer searched in vain and stood up rubbing his eyes.

'I can't see it. I'm not sure I could see anything.'

Westphal shrugged and nodded, closed up the periscope handles and signalled to the rating to lower the periscope.

'We're going to have to make some changes, von Bayer. There are a whole series of sandbanks along this piece of coast. The Four Fathoms Sand Ridge and then the Boulder Banks. I'd hoped to be able to make my way through the channel between them, but the British sowed new mines two nights ago according to our people. That closes the channels as far as I am concerned. That means that I shall have to lie off the coast outside the Stephenson Shoal, three and a half kilometres off shore. A longer journey for your people than we reckoned on. I'm going to take a risk. I'll let two of my men go with you. Experienced seamen. They'll get you there. Help you unload and bring the dinghy back. I'll let you have a trailer dinghy for your stores. You'll have to destroy that.'

'Shall we be able to land where I wanted?'

'More or less, give or take a kilometre.'

Von Bayer looked at his watch. It was just after midnight GMT. He looked back at Westphal.

'How long have I got before we start?'

'Thirty minutes provided there are no new problems.'

'I'll get my people ready.'

Von Bayer stood checking the list as Westphal's crewmen passed the team's stores up the ladder to the conning-tower. The big flange had been folded back and he could smell the salt sea air. When the last package had gone up he went up the ladder himself and joined Westphal on the curved deck of the submarine. The night air was cold but refreshing after the fetid air inside the U-boat, and the deck was far higher out of the water than he had expected. Two rope ladders curved from the deck to the dinghies, and everywhere was silent except for the wind in the stays and the slap of waves against the hull.

His team came up one by one, the girl last, and then Westphal said, 'Good luck,' and he was lying face down on the curve of the hull, his feet feeling clumsily for the wooden slats of the ladder. The dinghies were ten feet lower than the deck and von Bayer moved each foot carefully until a strong hand gripped his ankle guiding it to the next slat, and then the next. Seconds later the soft booming slap of a wave soaked him to the skin, and hands helped him into the dinghy.

As the crewmen cast off, the dinghies surged away from the U-boat on the tide, and both sailors were using the oars to keep them on course. Even when his eyes grew accustomed to the dark, von Bayer could see nothing ahead of them as they sank and lifted in the long reach of the waves. Twenty centimetres of sea water covered the canvas floor of the dinghy, washing up the back of his legs as he sat with both hands gripping the stiff rope handles at the edge of the dinghy. The sky was almost cloudless, a solid blue-black expanse with the moon an oversize golden disc hanging low, and shedding its yellow light on their anxious, upturned faces. Only Kleist looked back at him. With a half-smile on his lips, Kleist winked at him. And for the first time he could hear the creak of the leather bands round the oars straining in their rowlocks as the sailors leaned against the oars. Von Bayer could hear the thud of the waves now on the long stretches of the beach. He knew from the Sea-Lion report that the beaches here were sandy, with dunes behind that gave on to a small metalled road that served the holiday chalets at Camber village. Then, almost in one movement, the two sailors were in the water up to their chests, running and stumbling as they dragged on the ropes and the dinghy skated on the surface of the shallow water to grind up on to the wet sand.

One by one they scrambled out, jumping into the shallow water, Schultz and Kruger helping the sailors drag the first dinghy up the beach. The second dinghy was swinging broadside on to the waves and only the solid weight of the stores prevented it from capsizing. When both dinghies had been dragged clear of the sea the stores were unloaded and carried up to the edge of the dry sand of the dunes. Fifteen minutes later the sailors had thrust off to the ebb tide and in minutes they were out of sight.

In the bright moonlight von Bayer moved his team up to the tall grass of the dunes. He sent Voss off to do a quick reconnaissance. He had studied the maps as often as von Bayer himself. He knew the area of the Camber beach was not mined because there had been reports from Luftwaffe pilots that they had seen horses being exercised in the early mornings. Possibly from a yeomanry regiment that had been identified at Rye.

Voss came back ten minutes later and sat down alongside von Bayer. He put his mouth to von Bayer's ear.

'All the holiday chalets are empty. There's barbed wire round the fences and a notice saying "Mines." There are no mines and the sand is full of footprints. There's an empty shop, a wooden shack where we could put the stores. The first two chalets are still furnished. We could use them, but no lights.'

'Did you go to the end of the chalets?'

'Yes. They're all deserted.'

'Get Kruger and Schultz, and put the stores in the shop. I'll take the other two to the first chalet. You join us as soon as you've finished.'

Voss touched the two men and waved them after him. Von Bayer took Kleist and Ushi down a break in the dunes and out on to the narrow metalled road. He stood with his arm barring the way, in the shadow of the dunes, watching the road. Then they ran across the exposed road to the rolls of Dannert wire, following along them until they ended by the gate of the first chalet. There was a kitchen window ajar at the back and von Bayer put in his arm and reached down for the handle, then opened the window over the kitchen sink. As it opened he clambered over the window-sill, into the sink and then jumped to the floor. Seconds later he had opened the back door for Kleist and the girl.

The furnishings were sparse: deck-chairs, a couple of card tables, and two wicker chairs. But there was crockery and cutlery in plenty, and cooking pots and pans, a small electric grill and boiling ring. Von Bayer took out all the electric light bulbs and then switched on the mains switch under the stairs. The grill was warm a few seconds later. He switched it off. Upstairs there were bunk beds for four and a child's cot. No water ran when he turned on the taps.

They sat in the small parlour waiting for the others to come back.

Kleist said softly, 'Well, Max, we're here. It's hard to believe.'

Von Bayer shrugged. 'Not for me. This is only the start.' He turned to look at the girl. 'I'll want you to go into Rye with me tomorrow. I want to get some kind of vehicle.'

She looked back at him. 'I'm scared, Max.'

Von Bayer smiled back at her. 'No you're not. You're nervous. We all are.'

'Are you?'

'No. But I'm at home in this country. It's easier for me.'

He looked back at Kleist. 'How do you feel, Walter?'

Kleist shrugged and smiled. 'Wet, cold, wishing I was back at Schloss Eger playing "*Ich schenk' mein Herz*".'

Von Bayer laughed softly. 'We'll be back soon, Walter.'

The big brown eyes looked at him. 'You are thinking of going back, then?'

'Of course.'

'How?'

'Kästner will fix that for us.'

Then the others were back. Schultz was looking angry. 'You'd better tell Kruger that he does what he's told.'

'What's happened, Otto?'

'Look.' He turned and pointed to where a smiling Kruger was carrying a thin black cat.

'She's just a stray, Herr Sturmbannführer. She'll bring us good luck.'

'Rudi, there's no water in the taps. Find the turncock and turn it on so that we can have a drink and something to eat.'

'Yes, sir.'

Eleven

Von Bayer was wearing a tweed sports coat and grey flannels, and he and the girl walked hand in hand along the road to Rye. Past the golf course and its deserted club-house, and across the little hump-backed bridge over the River Rother. They turned left at the main road and over the other side of the big bridge he could see the shops.

The garage stood back from the main road. A man was watching them as they walked towards the little glassed-in office. There was a poster stuck on the side window that asked, 'Is your journey really necessary?' Von Bayer pushed open the office door and a bell rang in the workshop. An elderly man in blue overalls came through to the small office.

'G'morning, sir. What can I do for you?'

'Have you got a car for sale?'

The man screwed up his face and pushed his cap to the back of his head as he scratched his forehead.

'Depends what you wanted. I've got a 1937 baby Austin, a nearly new Anglia, and a biggish 1936 Standard.'

'Could I see them?'

'Sure. They're in the workshop. If I leave 'em outside the sea air don't do 'em no good.'

He led them through the office into the ancient workshop. He switched on a light and tugged the dust-cloths off the three cars.

'The baby Austin's very sound but you'll get ten gallons basic with the Standard and that's bin chauffeur maintained.

The old girl bought it from me four years ago and it's only done six thousand miles.'

'Can you recommend it?'

'Oh yes. You couldn't fault it. But you'll need black-out shields for the headlights. She ain't used it since the war started.'

'How much is it?'

'Is it cash or hire-purchase?'

'Cash.'

'Call it a hundred and ten quid then and I'll throw in the shields.'

'Can you fit them while I go to the bank?'

'Sure, it's a ten-minute job.'

'And petrol?'

The old man smiled. 'I've got last month's coupons as well. I'll fill her up for you, and then you've still got ten gallons for November. OK?'

'That's fine. We'll be back in fifteen minutes.'

As they walked up the hill into the town the girl said, 'Why didn't you pay him straight away?'

'Nobody normally carries that much cash around with them. And talk of the bank makes him feel we're not strangers.'

'I thought he'd see me shaking.'

Von Bayer laughed and took her hand. 'Just pretend you really *are* English. That's what I do. I'm an Englishman. Medically unfit with high blood-pressure.'

'Have you really got high blood-pressure, Max?'

He laughed. 'I have when I hold my breath.'

They walked up to the cobbled square, past the church and then von Bayer froze. Across the square he saw the blue and white sign outside the police station. A sergeant was standing on the steps staring at them. Von Bayer squeezed the girl's hand and walked round the square towards the police station. At the steps he halted. 'Excuse me, but could you tell me where I can find Cook's Garage?'

The constable came down the steps and pointed back the way they had come.

'Across the square, down the hill, under the archway and it's on the left, just before the bridge.'

'Thank you, officer.'

The girl saw the beads of perspiration on von Bayer's face as they walked back across the square.

'That was careless. Stupid,' he said quietly.

The car was waiting for them. As they drove through Rye to the Camber road he said, 'You must go on net tonight at nine. Kästner will be anxious for news.'

'What's next?'

'I want to drive into Tenterden this afternoon and see if I can rent a cottage or a farmhouse.'

'Where?'

'Somewhere towards Cranbrook.'

'What about the place you planned? The bombed place.'

'I think it's too near the coast. We can find better than that.'

They parked the car at the near end of the row of chalets and walked down towards the far end. There was no noise except for the sea, and the chalet looked as deserted as the rest of them. Only von Bayer noticed the flash of sun as the gun barrel moved at the upstairs window.

It was Voss at the window and the others were stripping and cleaning the two sub-machine-guns that Voss had 'borrowed' from his Wehrmacht sources. They were both Thomsons, captured at Dunkirk.

He had made a trial run at the first estate agent's in the tree-lined High Street in Tenterden. But there seemed to be no restriction on living in the defence zone. At the second estate agency he was more specific, and the woman clerk pulled out several files from the cabinet. He looked carefully at the photographs and details of the four properties she offered him. He handed three back to her and re-read the fourth.

It was called Cragg's Farm and it was on the road to Cranbrook. It was a five-bedroomed farmhouse with two barns.

'How much is the rent for Cragg's Farm?'

'Well it *was* five pounds a week, but it's been on the

market now for nearly a year. We're authorized to accept any reasonable offer.'

'Would four pounds a week be acceptable for a three months' let?'

'There is one snag. The Robinsons who own it used to farm Cragg's Farm themselves. They decided to sell their farmland to the Parkins and just keep the house. Part of the deal was that the Parkins could use the access road to move their cows twice a week. Would you find that objectionable?'

Von Bayer frowned and then smiled. 'Not if it's only twice a week. When could we move in?'

'The rent is monthly in advance. You could go in right away. There would be a ten-pound deposit against damage to furniture and chattels. We can give you the keys right now.'

'Are the furnishings reasonable?'

'They're very nice. You can inspect the house first, of course.'

Von Bayer counted out sixty-two pounds and the clerk gave him a receipt and three keys on a piece of thick sisal. The label said, 'Cragg's Farm/Robinson.'

They drove west from Tenterden and turned right from the Hastings Road. The road twisted between high hedges and the verges had obviously not been cut since the war started. They stood high with the dried heads of cow parsley and hogweed.

They nearly passed the small wooden sign that said 'Cragg's Farm'. It was almost hidden by tufts of thick grass, and it pointed to the wide opening where a five-barred gate stood open. The gate itself was overhung with holly, and had obviously not been closed for years. The driveway was rutted and poached from the cattle, and from the road to the farmhouse it was almost a quarter of a mile, rising gently to where the house stood at the crest of the hill.

The farmhouse was brick-built, solid and four-square, unpretentious and strangely friendly. The thin October sunlight caught the leaded lights of the windows and the small wicket gate that led into the small garden swung slowly in the slight breeze. They walked up to the solid oak door. The second key opened it and they walked inside.

It was eight o'clock when they got back to the chalet at Camber. A police constable had ridden slowly by on a bicycle early in the afternoon and an army dispatch-rider had gone past on the main road on a motor-cycle an hour earlier. They had noticed that he wore an arm-band with blue and white stripes. Kruger identified the motor-bike as a 500 cc BSA. 'Royal Corps of Signals,' von Bayer said.

There was coffee for them in the thermos, and a slab of cold corned-beef. After they had eaten and told the others about the farmhouse, von Bayer and the girl went to the smaller of the two bedrooms. He pulled the radio out from under the bed and Ushi slackened the aerial screw. Kruger had laced an aerial up to the ceiling and round four sides of the picture-rail. Von Bayer wrote out a very brief message. They had agreed that the call-sign to Kästner should be repeated Ks and for von Bayer, repeated Bs. Kästner had warned him that his Morse was very rusty, but Ushi had given him some practice so that she could recognize his 'hand'. His message to Kästner merely confirmed that they had arrived according to plan.

At 8.55 p.m. Ushi Lange slid the clumsy headphones over her ears and touched the side of the set to check that it was warm. Her eyes went to the big tuning dial and she touched it without moving it. She looked down at the small pad with von Bayer's message written out in capitals. They were using a plus one code. It was worthless in terms of security: more boys' comic stuff rather than military, but they had finally decided that they couldn't bring themselves to transmit in clear, and the only coding facilities they could have laid hands on were too complicated for them to operate. Their code just shifted every letter on one place: A=B, B=C, etc. Figures were not to be coded. No names would be used of people or their locations.

Von Bayer checked his watch and then nodded. He watched the needle on the meter flickering backwards and forwards as Ushi operated the key. She stopped and turned the switch to receive, and they both waited, tense and apprehensive. Only seconds later von Bayer saw the needle flickering vigorously, and Ushi was smiling as she scribbled on the pad. She switched back a minute or two later to transmit and von Bayer watched her face as her eyes went from the pad to the flickering needle as she tapped out his first message. When she switched again to receive she reached for the pencil and started writing. Von Bayer waited impatiently. It seemed to be going on far too long. The messages were meant to be brief. Fortunately there was no risk from receiving, only from transmitting. Page after page were filled so he knew that it wasn't just Kästner's slow Morse. The curtains were closed and they were only using a torch, and the golden light made the girl's face look tanned and healthy as if she had just returned from holiday, and for a moment von Bayer was moved by the girl's devotion to Kleist. She was young and beautiful and talented. She could have survived so easily in Hamburg, working at the radio station and singing in the club at night. There would have been plenty of men willing to care for Ushi Lange. Instead she sat crouched in a chilly shack taking down Morse from a man in Berlin. And in her handbag was an identity card that said she was Ursula Long from Newcastle. Her address, a house that was known to have been destroyed in a Luftwaffe raid.

Then she put down the pad, switched to transmit, tapped a few characters on the Morse-key, switched off the set and shook her long, blonde hair as she pulled off the headphones.

'My God, Max,' she said. 'These phones are so old-fashioned. They weigh a ton.'

She handed him the sheets of the pad, and then the pad and pencil for him to decode the message. He looked at her face for a moment and said softly, 'I'm glad you came with us, Ushi. Somehow you keep us civilized without even trying. Thanks.'

He saw tears at the edge of her eyes and she said. 'I'd give a leg, an arm, both, if only Walter could be made well. I love him so much.'

'I know, Ushi. I love someone like that.' He reached out and put his hand on hers. 'I care about you, Ushi. Both of you.'

With tears on her cheeks she stood up and left him.

It took him fifteen minutes to transpose his first message from Kästner and when he had finished he read it again and again. Shivering.

The message said: 'BBB STOP CONGRATULATIONS STOP REGRET HAVING INFORM YOU GIRL FROM VILLAGE RAPED AND BRUTALIZED YOUR PARTY'S LAST NIGHT AT SE STOP SUSPECT ANSWERS FULLY DESCRIPTION YOUR OS STOP POLICE ENQUIRIES INSTITUTED LIABLE CAUSE PROBLEMS STOP TAKE PRECAUTIONS YOUR END STOP GOOD LUCK KKK MESSAGE ENDS'

He switched off the torch to save the battery and sat in the dark. He remembered going to Otto Schultz's room and seeing that the bed had not been slept in. And Schultz's pale, haggard face when he had found him sitting in the car before they started the long journey to Brest. It seemed years ago but it was less than a week. He wondered if the police inquiries had led to Schloss Eger. He had left no message, no letter, for his father. He had sensed the latent violence in Schultz from the moment he first met him and he knew in his heart that he had subconsciously seen that as an advantage. A plus not a minus. He screwed up each sheet of the pad and slid them into his pocket. He knew that despite this message he still saw Schultz's violence as a plus not a minus. They were in this chalet because he himself had planned violence. That was why they were all there. To do violence.

He walked slowly downstairs. In the small room he flashed his torch for a moment with his hand over the head. He bent down and shook Schultz and Kruger awake.

'Come and help me load the stores into the car.'

Twelve

Signalman Knight, despite his lowly rank, had, in civilian life, been a lecturer in Philosophy at the Sorbonne. At Oxford he had made a name, both as undergraduate and Fellow, for his theories on the relationship between the Cartesians and the Occasionists. But at the Sorbonne, as an Englishman, he lectured routinely on Descartes and his contemporaries. Being a Francophile he found French chauvinism particularly disappointing. He had joined the British Army as a volunteer immediately after the fall of France and his double-first in French and German had led him to his present situation in a caravan at Bosham just outside Chichester.

After a ghastly six months at Catterick Camp in Yorkshire he had acquired sufficient technical knowledge to operate the radio equipment used by Signals Security in their various enterprises.

One of the misfortunes of the Vichy French in Madagascar was that all their cable communications with Metropolitan France were routed through a cable link in Nairobi, Kenya; and before their cables were transmitted to France they were scrutinized by the Intelligence authorities in England. Signalman Knight was one of those authorities. He examined coded and decoded cables before onward transmission, and noted interesting and potentially interesting aspects of their contents. Knowing that they were subject to censorship, the senders kept the contents of their cables to straightforward commercial details, or used what they considered involved codes that passed a pleasant five minutes for the London decoders. But even routine commercial transactions can contain the germs of information useful to a country involved in total war. A mind that could sort out the relationships between Descartes and the Occasionists was ideal for probing these potential sources of information. Ships' documents from a merchant in Diego Suarez to his bank in Paris gave valuable information to the Royal Navy prowling in the Indian Ocean.

In boring interludes on particularly boring nights Signalman Knight found no relief in those pleasures that relieved his technician fellow soldiers. *Lilliput* and *Men Only* were not for him. This hiatus sometimes led Signalman Knight to unauthorized indulgences. These ranged from monitoring frequencies not in his remit, or even spitefully revenging himself on French chauvinism by varying, by large amounts, the monies transferred by Frenchmen in Madagascar to their banks in Paris or Lyons.

On this particular night he had monitored a brief period of signal traffic on a frequency that had once been used by the German Intelligence services. He had idly noted down the transmissions that were in hesitant, laboured Morse. Gazing at them afterwards he was amused by the naïveté of the one-letter shift code and had transposed the letters to keep himself awake. With no great interest he translated the German text. The format was odd. Certainly not military or naval, they were more like telegrams between individuals. Almost 'Having a lovely time. Wish you were here' kind of stuff. But who sends chatty notes to whom about rape? He doodled with anagrams of the three B's and K's and SE and OS but nothing came. The other odd thing was that one operator was obviously a professional and the other was an obvious beginner.

Signalman Knight was a conscientious soldier and wrote out a report, including the messages, and sent them with the usual returns with the Signals Don R from 7 Div the following morning to his masters in Croydon.

They had received a similar but untranslated text of the

same radio traffic from the Brigade I.O. of an armoured brigade stationed in Ashford, Kent. That report gave a signal strength of R7 as against Signalman Knight's view that the strength was no more than R5s. Both reports were sent to the Signals Evaluation Unit on the top floor of Peter Robinson's store at Oxford Circus. They were endorsed as low priority.

It had taken three trips over two days to move the stores and his team from Camber to the farmhouse, but von Bayer's morale was high. He had been stopped by an army patrol at a temporary road-block at Wittersham. His identity card, medical certificate and the Cragg's Farm address had got them through with no problems. But they had siphoned out a bottle of his petrol and held it up to the light before pouring it back in the car's tank and screwing on the cap. He couldn't understand why they had done that.

Von Bayer had walked about fifty yards from the farmhouse to where a small stand of oaks marked the high point of the surrounding farmland. From the garden the whole area down to the lane was clearly visible and from where he stood, under the trees, the fields rolled smoothly down to meet similar gentle slopes at least two miles away. Except for one small fold of dead ground to the north the whole area surrounding the house was commanded by the view from the bedroom windows.

There was the sparkle of frost on the fallen leaves and alongside the hedges of the fields, but there was no hardness to the ground. It was ten o'clock and the mist that had filled the valley was already lifting. The sky was blue and cloudless, but it was the pale blue of autumn. He stood with his hands in his trouser pockets and wondered if he dare send either of the two other English speakers out on his own. It would be stupid to think of using the girl on her own, but she could be good cover for one of the men. A couple were always less suspect than a man on his own. It had better be Kleist and Ushi.

They were gathered around the big kitchen table with the map and the two photographs. Voss looked up as von Bayer walked in.

'What are these markings round some of the buildings, Max?'

Von Bayer bent over to look at Voss's pointing finger.

'These maps were specially printed for Operation Sea-Lion. They are the English Ordnance Survey Maps, one inch to the mile. The buildings with mauve outlines round them were to be occupied by the Wehrmacht as soon as they were overrun. Those marked with red outlines were to be taken over on behalf of the Protectorate Government when required. What have you decided between you?'

Voss smiled. 'We're still arguing. The only thing we have agreed is that we don't go in from the seaward side.'

Von Bayer nodded. 'It could be done from that side but that's where they will expect an attack to come from – from the sea. Where are you putting the explosives?'

He shook his head at Schultz to stop him from answering.

Voss said, 'My suggestion was, against the wall of the generator shack.'

Von Bayer looked at Kruger. 'And you, Rudi?'

'I think against the operations shed.'

Von Bayer turned to the girl. 'You *know* where it should go don't you, Ushi?'

'The pylons.'

'Right. The point is that all the buildings are wood and that gives too little blast inside. Apart from that, this radar station has been attacked several times by the Luftwaffe. They can put those bits and pieces together in a couple of days. If we can bring down a pylon it's going to take much longer for them to get back on the air. Look.'

He leaned over the table and put the two photographs side by side.

'These three taller pylons carry the transmission aerials and those four carry the receiver aerials. Only the transmitter aerials matter. Without those they are not operational.' He looked up at Schultz. 'Can we do it, Otto? Can we fetch a tower down?'

'Are the bases concrete?'

'Yes. But I don't know how thick.'

'That doesn't matter. The thicker the better. Do we need the tower right down?'

'Yes.'

'We can do it, but it's going to take a quarter or even a third of our explosives.'

'For each tower? Von Bayer looked anxious.

'No. For all of them.'

Von Bayer smiled. 'You're a beautiful man, Otto Schultz. A beautiful man. Show me how we do it.'

Schultz had marked the photographs where he would want the charges placed. And then they spent two hours discussing how to get into the installation, the time they would need inside the wire and how they would get away. They decided everything except how they would get away. Kleist and von Bayer would decide that.

They drove down to Rye together that afternoon and left the car at Cook's Garage.

'She going all right, sir?' the old man asked.

'Beautifully, thank you. Could you put a couple of gallons in for me?'

Von Bayer pulled out the logbook and the book of coupons.

The old man winked. 'Leave it to me, sir.'

They walked round the bottom road to the small harbour area and along the narrow sea-wall. They could see the towers but they were too far away for them to see any details of the perimeter defences or the buildings. They walked up Mermaid Street and walked across to the far corner, past the police station and down a small cobbled slope. North of the site, along the seaward face, von Bayer could see the two lines of grass that were paler and browner than the rest of the grass. There were no similar lines on the other three sides. A small army pick-up van was parked just inside the perimeter wire alongside what looked like a small wooden guard hut. A soldier in battle-dress guarded the entrance. They didn't linger but walked briskly back to the garage.

The old man said, 'I've put three gallons in. That's a quid.'

Von Bayer realized that his petrol was black-market. The normal price of Pool petrol was 1/6d a gallon. He thanked the old man and gave him twenty-five shillings.

Out of curiosity von Bayer drove through the back lanes to check where the bombed farmhouse was that he had originally planned to use.

It looked just as the photographs had shown it. Gaunt, with its window frames empty; and a heap of rubble was all that was left of its back wall. He drove on into Appledore and turned left on to the Tenterden road. When they eventually arrived back at the farmhouse von Bayer switched off the engine and sat in silence. It was several minutes before he spoke.

'We can do it, Walter. They are not expecting any kind of attack except from the air. We've got to do the maximum damage because any move against the installation will mean really tight security afterwards.'

'You saw the anti-aircraft guns under the camouflage nets, Max?'

'Yes.' He turned to look at Kleist, smiling. 'Are you thinking what I'm thinking?'

'It would save explosive, and it would be a magnificent gesture to put it out of action with their own guns.'

Von Bayer laughed. 'We'd better stick to our plan.'

He told the others about what they had seen, and told them that they would carry out the attack the following night. Ushi Lange would stay behind at the farmhouse.

The next morning they had gone over the details again and again, but whatever refining of the plan they made, Kruger, Kleist and Schultz were going to need twelve minutes minimum to place the explosives. And they would have to double up the fuse length if they were to have any chance of getting away. Kruger would leave the site first and have the car ready to move off as the others were checked back by von Bayer.

Just before they set off von Bayer heard on the BBC News that Roosevelt had been re-elected President of the USA for a third term.

It was seven-thirty when they arrived on the outskirts of Rye. Von Bayer gave them directions over the bridge and they left the car in the shadow of the timber store. Von Bayer went ahead with Schultz and Voss, Kleist and Kruger followed together. With the moon not yet up they stumbled slowly along the narrow pathway that skirted the radar station. It took almost an hour before they were on the east side of the perimeter. There they huddled together in the cold autumn air.

Not long after ten they heard anti-aircraft fire far away in the direction of Hythe, and shortly after they heard the steady beat of heavy bombers flying in from the Channel. They were on a line that would take them to the Midlands. Far back behind them searchlights were sweeping the sky and they could hear the rattle of the machine-guns of the fighter escort taking on the night-fighters attacking the bombers. Then all was silent again. Suddenly the silence was broken with the sound of the air-raid sirens in the town.

The second wave of bombers was coming in, and von Bayer said softly, 'OK. We go now.'

They crouched low as they stumbled across the tussocky grass and at the perimeter wire von Bayer threw himself down and, lying prone, cut through the two bottom lines of barbed wire and with a gloved hand lifted it up. Schultz was through first, followed by Kruger who pulled the wire higher for Kleist to roll under. The moon was up now, and von Bayer and Voss could see the latticed structures of the two nearest towers. They knelt with their Tommy-guns resting on their knees. Von Bayer looked at his watch. They had only been gone three minutes but it seemed like an hour. Then the bombers were overhead. They heard a shout and the anti-aircraft guns they had seen on their reconnaissance were firing in pairs, and seconds later they could hear the whirr of shrapnel about thirty feet away.

The three men laid the charges as Schultz had ordered and Schultz himself had connected the detonators. And it was he who climbed the lattice on each tower to plant the auxiliary charge ten feet above the concrete. The noise of his breathing and his boots on the steel work seemed frightening to Kleist and Kruger. As Schultz came down the last tower he trailed the fuses in different directions and then put in a secondary line that linked all three main charges.

Schultz pulled Kruger's face near his. 'Off to the car now. I'll bring Kleist with me. Three minutes.' Without waiting for an answer he slid off his jacket and held it over the first fuse. The fuse caught the flame from his lighter instantly, and Schultz blew on it sharply and cursed softly when it sparked. He found Kleist at the fuse of the middle tower and sent him on his way. He had to cut the third fuse again but it lit the second time and then he was running, crouched, back to the wire. The all-clear went as he ducked under the wire.

There was a sharp wind blowing now and Schultz cursed in case it speeded up the burning fuse. He took Kleist's arm and they stumbled together after the dark shapes of von Bayer and Voss. They all lay panting in the thick grass at the edge of the road and a few minutes later Kruger was there with the car.

Von Bayer slid in next to Kruger and when the others were in and the doors closed he said, 'Back to the bridge and turn right to the minor road. Then fast as you can go.' He turned to Schultz. 'How long now, Otto?'

'Seven minutes.'

Von Bayer turned back. 'There, Rudi. Now left and fast.'

Five minutes later they were at the bombed farmhouse.

'Up the drive at the side, Rudi. Right up so that we're under the trees.' He looked at his watch. 'Two minutes to go, Otto.'

And as he spoke they heard it. And Schultz said, 'It was that bloody wind getting up. It was fanning the fuse.'

Von Bayer turned to look at him. 'How did it sound, Otto?'

Schultz grinned. 'It sounded like our Walter on the piano, bloody marvellous.'

Von Bayer wondered how long it would be before they found the clue he had left them. An Irish passport in the name of O'Keefe. It had been one of his requests to Kästner, and was genuine although its owner was long since dead. Von Bayer had seen the reports of the negotiations with the IRA men who had gone to Berlin for money, arms, and encouragement. And he had read their own comments on the bombings they had carried out in England since the start of the war.

All night they sat in the car. It had been light for an hour before they set off down the lane. Von Bayer wanted a sporting chance of seeing road blocks before they got to them. He drove the car himself and when they got to Tenterden, the small town seemed to be going about its business quite normally.

They were back at the farm at Cranbrook by ten-thirty, Von Bayer shaved and then drove to the telephone kiosk at the small green by the cross-roads. He put the coins in the box and dialled the number. He pressed the 'A' button and waited as it rang. Then he recognized the old man's voice.

'Is that Cook's Garage?'

'Yes. Joe Cook speaking.'

'Morning, Mr Cook. I bought the Standard from you. I was wondering if I could bring her in for you to check the carburettor. She's a bit sluggish.'

'Not today, sir. You can't get in. They've blocked off the main road and the Winchelsea road. The air-raid last night.'

'I hope there wasn't too much damage.'

'The buggers knocked down two of the towers from what I can gather.'

'I'll try again tomorrow, Mr Cook.'

'All right then. She maybe needs the filter cleanin'.'

Every night they had contacted Kästner with a nil report but that night von Bayer wrote out his brief report with schoolboy enthusiasm.

KKK STOP SUGGEST HGS BOYS LOOK AT TARGET TWO STOP BBB

There had only been a routine acknowledgement.

Kleist and von Bayer were drinking coffee and reading the *Kent Messenger.* Half each.

They both looked up when Rudi Kruger rushed into the room.

'There's a car coming up the drive.'

Kleist went back upstairs with Kruger, and von Bayer called out to Ushi to join him.

The knock on the door was loud and peremptory. Von Bayer opened it. The woman who stood there was wearing a brown tweed suit, a brown pullover and pearls, brown brogue shoes and a close-fitting felt hat. She was about fifty years old but her angular face had a clear complexion and her grey eyes were quite beautiful.

'I'm afraid I don't know your name but my name is Waring. Patsy Waring from The Barn House, just up the road. I'm collecting, and I thought I'd call. I hope it's convenient.'

Von Bayer smiled. 'Of course. Come in.'

She stepped inside and walked through to the sitting-room without further invitation. She stopped when she saw Ushi Lange.

Von Bayer said, 'Let me introduce you, this is Ursula Long. Ursula this is Mrs Waring.' He turned to the woman. 'It is Mrs, isn't it?'

'Oh, yes.'

She looked at von Bayer. 'I heard that a couple had moved in to Cragg's so I thought I should say hello.'

'Do sit down, Mrs Waring.'

She sat down in one of the easy chairs, looking round the room as she did so.

'I see the Robinsons have taken their china with them. Some of us had wondered just a teeny bit. It was Meissen you know, made for the Kaiser. Not *really* the best of taste in these times, d'you know.'

Von Bayer was smiling and Mrs Waring said, 'You must meet my husband, Hugo. He's at the War Office, gets down here once a fortnight. Now . . .' she said, as if von Bayer had been wasting time, 'now to the collection.' She smiled, an acid, practised smile. 'It's two collections really, one for the Red Cross and the other's the Spitfire fund. The WI have made a rule, a pound limit for the gentry and a couple of bob for the rest. Hugo says, with the Germans on our doorstep so

to speak, it's up to us chaps in the danger area to give gener-
ously. I'm sure you agree.'

Von Bayer took out two pound notes from his wallet.

'I think your husband's quite right, Mrs Waring. We must
support the war effort in every way we can.'

'You're not local, Mr er . . .'

'Barnes. Max Barnes. No, I come from the Cambridge area.'

She stood up. 'Ah well. I mustn't linger. You must have a
bite with us one of these days.'

After she had gone Ushi Lange said, 'You were fantastic,
Max.'

He smiled. 'I'm used to those sorts of ladies, Ushi. They're
no problem.'

In one of the old-fashioned bedrooms in the 'Mermaid' in
Rye, Major Hastings, Royal Engineers, and Captain Phillips, Intelligence Corps, sat looking at the small collection of
oddments on the coffee table. Hastings sat on the edge of the
bed. It was his room. Phillips sat in the tapestry chair fanning the smoke from Hastings' pipe away from his face. He
pushed his hair from his eyes as he spoke.

'I know it adds up, George, but they haven't attacked a
military target before.'

Hastings shrugged. 'You've got a Republic of Ireland
passport. Your people confirm that it's not a forgery. The
detonator caps were German-made. Your people confirm
that the IRA have had people in Berlin. They're there for
money, arms and ammunition, and a bit of specialist advice.
Surely that's enough. It's the bloody Micks all right.'

'But why this type of target? It's a lot different from killing old ladies with bombs at Victoria Station.'

'Sure, but they've had help from the krauts. They're getting more ambitious.'

'If you'd wanted to wreck the towers, where would you
have put the explosives?'

Hastings shrugged. 'Exactly where *they* put it.'

Phillips sighed. 'Why didn't the third tower come right
down like the other two?'

'God knows. The charges were in the same place. Maybe they economized. Got short of gelignite. Or were in a hurry. Probably frightened by the bombers.'

'Nothing you would criticize as being unprofessional?'

'Not really. What's on your mind?'

Phillips looked at him. 'Could it have been the Jerries themselves? Some sort of commando group. In and out.'

'Were there any sightings of boats at that time?'

'No. But their E-boats get across the Channel frequently. They landed two agents at Dymchurch a month ago. We picked 'em up the next morning. They came by E-boat and we had no reports on either the landing or the boat.'

'How did you get on to them?'

'They barely spoke English and were very low-grade. One of them went into a pub in Hythe, at eight in the morning, and asked for a large whisky.'

Hastings laughed. 'Even that sounds more like the Micks than the Germans.'

'Is there anything that would have convinced you that this was the Jerries?'

'Yep. If they'd used plastic explosive.'

Phillips stood up. 'You're probably right. Are you going back to London?'

'No. I'm going to Ashford.'

Ushi Lange and Max von Bayer walked slowly, hand-in-hand, along the edge of the ploughed field. When the shower started they stood under the shelter of a chestnut tree. Its brown and yellow leaves spread from the edge of the wood and drifted across the furrows of the rich, dark soil. A few leaves still clung to the branches and the two of them made themselves comfortable, sitting with their backs against the massive trunk. As they sat there three fighter planes came over the top of the woods at the far end of the field. The girl shaded her eyes with her hand as she looked up.

'Are those Spitfires, Max?'

'No, they're Hurricanes. This is 615 Squadron.'

'What's the difference?'

'The Spitfires have rounded wing-ends, the Hurricanes

are square-cut. They've got a much lower ceiling than the Spitfires.'

The Hurricanes were soon far away but they could see a quick flash as they banked and turned against the pale grey of the clouds. There was a rainbow over the woods as they walked back to the lane. The car was parked at the edge of the woods. Not hidden, but not conspicuous. As they turned the corner the girl gasped and her hand gripped von Bayer's tightly.

'Look,' she whispered.

There were two policemen standing by the car and a cycle was leaning against the fence along the woods. The bonnet of the car had been opened.

'Don't panic, Ushi. The standard story. You're my girl-friend, we're thinking of buying a place down here. A small-holding.'

'What's a smallholding?'

'Ein Kleinlandbesitz.'

Then they were at the car and von Bayer saw that there were two cycles and one of the policemen was a sergeant. It was the sergeant who looked up and spoke.

'This your car, sir?'

'Yes.'

'Have you got the logbook with you?'

'I have.'

He fished in his pocket and pulled out the logbook. The book of petrol coupons was inside it. He handed it over and the sergeant read the details in the logbook carefully, and then checked the coupons.

'Can I see your identity card?'

Von Bayer handed it over and watched the sergeant reading it slowly. Then, still holding all the documents, the sergeant said, 'And what are you doing down here, sir?'

'Looking for a house to buy.'

The sergeant's brown eyes looked him over, his tongue slowly exploring his bottom lip.

'Are you trying to help the Germans?'

'I don't understand, Sergeant.'

The sergeant pointed at the car's engine under the open bonnet.

'You're in a Defence Area. You know the regulations. You don't leave a car without demobilizing it. The distributor cap is on and the rotor-arm hasn't been removed.'

'That's very stupid of me. I saw a pheasant in the field and I stopped to take my girl back to see it. I didn't think.'

The sergeant hesitated for a moment and then handed back the documents.

'Where are you living now?'

'Just between Cranbrook and Tenterden.'

'They're both in the Defence Area. You ought to know better, sir. Don't do it again.'

'I certainly won't, Sergeant.'

The watching constable pulled down the bonnet and hooked on the clamps. The two policemen watched them drive off. Von Bayer kept his eyes to the front.

'Don't look back, Ushi, for God's sake.'

He skirted Ashford to the south and it took almost two hours for them to get back to the farmhouse.

Von Bayer signalled Kästner that night that they would be dealing with target number four in the next two days. Kästner's reply was full of congratulations, and it was obvious that he had been able to find out what had happened to the radar towers at target number two.

Thirteen

Von Bayer's sketches of the fighter airfield at Hawkinge, and its immediate surroundings, showed an area that was roughly one kilometre square. Lying diagonally, its north-east side bounded by the main road from Folkestone that ran through the village of Hawkinge itself. On the other three sides it was bounded by minor roads that carried little traffic apart from farm vehicles. They led nowhere except to the small farming hamlets of four or five cottages that huddled together haphazardly along their winding routes. To the north-west a cemetery with a crematorium had a chapel in its centre that was sometimes a useful marker for the trio of Messerschmitt-110s of Erprobungsgruppe 210 that special-ized in harassing the airfield at Hawkinge from their base in Calais-Marck.

At the side of the cemetery was a path which had been overgrown from two years' neglect. Twenty feet back from the road it was made impassable by a small forest of thick brambles. It was there that they parked the car.

Schultz and Kleist were the only ones who would be inside the perimeter apart from von Bayer. Their surveillance had shown that the despatch rider brought the last of the day's reports from the radar station at Lympne at 22:30 each evening. He was RASC not RAF, and the transport platoon was changed often enough for a new face to be quite normal. They had checked out the route. He usually came off the main road at the village of Newington and passed Dane Farm at about 22:10. From the bend in the road just beyond

Dane Farm there were no houses and no cottages, and it was there that von Bayer and Schultz were waiting. The night was sharp with frost and there was no sound except the far-away bellowing of a bulling cow.

Then, as they crouched in the hedge, Schultz held up a hand and whispered. 'I can hear him, he's coming.' And he snatched up the container and ran into the road, spreading the oil in a wide slick from verge to verge. Then they moved up about twenty yards in case the oil didn't work. The motor-cycle turned the corner, they could see the faint light from the slats of its headlamp guard. It was doing about forty miles an hour and the rider was crouched low as the front wheel touched the oil. For a few frantic seconds he fought the slide, but the front wheel had gone, and the foot-rest was fetching sparks from the metalled road. The engine raced as the bike went down on its side on top of the rider, his leg pinioned under the hot cylinder-block.

Von Bayer pulled up the exhaust lift to cut the engine and wheeled the motor-cycle into the shallow ditch. Schultz had one arm hooked round the corporal's neck and his fingers dug into the man's windpipe as his feet drummed on the ground. Then Kruger came panting down the road as the others were stripping the man of his uniform.

Von Bayer said to Schultz. 'When you've tied him up put him behind the hedge. But stuff his mouth well.'

The uniform was small for von Bayer, but he struggled into it, and the calf-length riding boots were comfortable enough. He went through all the pockets. There was an AB64 Part 11. A work-ticket for the journey. A wallet with two pounds and a photograph of a young woman with a baby on her lap and in a back flap a pornographic picture of a girl with two men. There was some loose change, a khaki handkerchief and two keys in the trouser pocket, and a regulation field dressing in the front pocket. The riding helmet was oversize and von Bayer shoved the khaki handkerchief around the frame to close it up.

Rudi Kruger looked him over as he sat astride the motor-cycle. He was holding von Bayer's clothes to take back to the car. He pointed at the controls and whispered. 'That's the brake, this is the clutch, it's a foot gear-shift and this is the accelerator on the twist grip. It's much the same as a BMW.'

Von Bayer saw Schultz struggling back through the hedge.

'Wait until you see me on the other side of the wire, Otto. It may take me some time. It depends on what happens.'

Schultz nodded and von Bayer kicked the engine alive and let in the clutch. Schultz and Kruger watched until the red tail-light was lost in the darkness, and then walked up the road together, Schultz said, 'He really is a cool bastard, our Max. He decides what's got to be done and he just does it. They knew what they were doing all right when they picked him for this little game.'

They were at the corner where Schultz had to leave him, and Kruger squeezed Schultz's arm. 'You're not so bad yourself, Otto. Best of luck.'

He watched Schultz for a few paces and then he too was lost in the darkness.

At the cemetery von Bayer had stopped and checked the two panniers at the back of the motor-cycle. There was a bundle of personal mail tied with string and two large buff envelopes.

He took a deep breath and rode on, turning right. Two hundred yards later he swung into the gateway and was stopped by the RAF policeman. He had a rifle hitched over his shoulder.

'AB64, mate.'

Von Bayer handed it over with the work-ticket inside. The policeman handed it back.

'You been here before corporal?'

'No.'

The RAF man turned, one hand holding the sling of his rifle, the other pointing into the darkness.

'Right ahead there's the Squadron office. You leave the official mail there. Get a signature from the flight-sergeant. The personal mail goes to Hut 4. Down the cinder track, past the Fire-post and it's the second hut on the left. No need for a signature, just hand it to anyone there.'

'Is there anywhere I can get a cup of tea?'

'Yeah. There's a NAAFI hut right at the end of the track. You'll hear the bloody noise.'

'Thanks.'

'Don't leave your engine running outside the Squadron hut. The old man sleeps there and he don't like being disturbed.'

Von Bayer nodded and let in the clutch. He stumbled up the wooden steps of the Squadron office. There was a black curtain inside the door and then he was in the office, his eyes screwed up against the sudden light.

There were two trestle tables and a sergeant sat at one of them, typing with two fingers on an ancient typewriter. For a moment he went on typing and von Bayer saw the silhouette sheets of Dorniers and Heinkels pinned up on the wall alongside a photograph of a naked girl. Then the sergeant looked up.

'Ah. Put the official mail down there.' He pointed to the corner of the table.

'I need a signature, Sergeant.'

'Flight-sergeant if you please, Corporal.'

'Flight-sergeant.'

'You got any personal mail for us?'

'Yes. I was told to take it to Hut 4.'

'All in good time, my friend. Where is it?'

'It's on my bike.'

'Just nip out and get it and I'll sign your little chit for you.'

When von Bayer went inside with the packet of personal mail the sergeant took it and slid off the string, reading the names and addresses on the envelopes. He took out two envelopes and handed the rest back.

'Here's your chit. These two are for me.'

'Thank you, Flight-sergeant.'

'You know how to find Hut 4?'

'Yes. The guard told me.'

Von Bayer found Hut 4 and handed the mail to a pilot officer wearing the ribbon of the DFC. Then he rode on until he was just short of the canteen. He swung the motor-cycle up on its stand and moved off quickly into the darkness. He was tempted to run but he knew that if he was stopped they'd be more suspicious if he was running.

For a few seconds he was afraid that Schultz and Kleist were in the wrong place, and then he saw Schultz's white face against the wire. He checked the ground at his feet and then reached out with the pliers. He took Kleist off to the armourers' shed and then came back for Schultz and took him across to the row of planes alongside the workshops.

He waited impatiently as Schultz ducked under the wing of the first Hurricane. Fifteen minutes later he walked him back to the wire and then went back for Kleist.

Back at the fence he whispered to Schultz. 'How long were they set for?'

'Like you said, twenty minutes.'

'Get back to the car and wait for me.'

'Don't be long, Max.'

Von Bayer walked back to the canteen and, kneeling, he pressed the plastic under the front corner of the wooden hut. He pressed in the detonator and the pencil-timer and stood up. Inside, raucous voices were singing. He couldn't make out the words but it was something about Methuselah.

He wheeled the motor-cycle away from the hut and started her up. He rode back slowly to the gate. The guard nodded to him as he went through and he turned left and headed up the road.

They were waiting for him at the cemetery with the car already at the edge of the road. He rode the motor-cycle past the car, up the rutted path, and shoved it into the brambles.

He slid into the passenger seat at the front of the car as Kleist started her up.

Just past Lyminge they stopped and got out. Listening. There were another two minutes to go. It was four minutes before they heard the explosions. Two almost together, four a few seconds apart and then one on its own.

Schultz laughed. 'Seven bangs and we only planted six.'

It took them six hours to get back to the farmhouse. Avoiding all main roads until they got to Tenterden, and sending someone ahead each time they crossed a main road.

Although they were exhausted they were all too excited to sleep, and after they had buried the uniform and papers under the floor of the smaller barn they sat around talking until the early afternoon.

Von Bayer had taken Ushi Lange with him into Cranbrook to buy food. He had registered them all at the same grocer and the same butcher but previously he had done the buying himself. He explained the coupon values to the girl as they drove to the small town, and left her to do the buying alone.

Rudi Kruger had found a chess-board and a box of draughts and he and Schultz sat on Kruger's bed talking and playing, still unable to sleep.

Schultz unwrapped one of his cigars. 'I've only got seven more of these bloody things left.'

'Maybe we can raid a tobacco shop, Otto.'

'It's not that that I want most.' Schultz grinned.

'What is it then?'

'I want a girl. I want a good screw.'

Kruger laughed. 'You won't find any brothels around here, Otto. This is farming country.'

'To hell with brothels. I never use 'em, not even in Berlin. There's always our sweet Ushi.'

Kruger looked up quickly. 'She's Walter's girl, Otto. You'd better not forget that.'

'I know, but she ain't getting it off our Walter, that's for sure. She's just being wasted.'

'Maybe that's how she wants it.'

'Just think what you could do to those beautiful tits of hers.'

'Oh for Christ's sake forget it. You need some sleep.'

'No. It's the excitement makes me want a woman all the more.'

'It's your move, Otto. You'd better have a cold bath.'

Schultz laughed and moved his piece on the board.

Von Bayer put the cardboard box with the food in it on the ground, and fished for the key to the car's boot. When he opened it he saw the rope there.

He hardly spoke on the journey back and when they got back to the farmhouse he hurried inside up to Schultz's bedroom. It was empty, and he went to the next room. Kruger's.

Schultz and Kruger looked up as he walked in.

'What did you use to tie up the despatch rider, Schultz?'

'He didn't need tying up, Max.'

'Why not?'

'He isn't gonna be any trouble.'

'You killed him?'

'Yeah. It's best that way.'

'Those weren't my orders.'

Schultz shruggled. 'We're all in this together, Max. That's what we came for, to kill the bastards.'

Von Bayer was white with anger. 'You are a stupid oaf, Schultz. The police, the army, everybody, will be hunting for us now.'

'They will in any case. When you put the plastic on that canteen hut you'll have killed a handful more than I did.'

'For God's sake, Otto. That could have been an in and out raid. They'll know now that whoever did it had had days to watch them. To check the despatch rider's route and times. They'll guess that we must still be around.'

Schultz stared back at him defiantly, puffing his cigar.

Von Bayer opened his mouth to speak and then changed his mind. But the look he gave Schultz as he turned to leave the room was message enough.

His long signal recording their success to Kästner that night did nothing to ease his tension. He decided that they would all rest the following day. They wouldn't even spend time planning. For the first time since the operation had started he felt uneasy. He knew exactly how to deal with types like Schultz on his own home ground. But in enemy territory it wasn't so easy. The lives of all of them depended on his planning and judgement. And Schultz was beginning to be a hazard to all of them. A day's rest would do them all good.

Captain Phillips had been promoted to Major, and with his new green Intelligence Corps crowns on his battle-dress shoulders, he got a 'Present arms!' instead of a slap on a rifle-butt as he walked into Hobart House. Major Hastings was waiting for him in Room 904.

'Congratulations.'

'Thanks. And thanks for the call. You didn't say what it was about.'

'Take a pew. Tea or coffee?'

'Tea, please.'

Hastings pressed the button on his internal phone and ordered tea for both of them. You could order tea if you had a visitor, otherwise you fetched it yourself. He settled back on his hard chair.

'You remember us looking at that sabotage at Rye. The radar station?'

'I certainly do.'

'I was called in to check on a sabotage thing at an RAF airfield in East Kent. Hawkinge in fact.'

'What happened?'

'Seven people killed. Twenty injured. A Hurricane completely written off, and two out of action for at least three weeks. A small ammunition store blown up, and sundry other buildings damaged.'

'And they used the same methods?'

'No, they didn't. That's why I called you.'

'Don't keep me in suspense.'

'They used plastic and pencil-timers. German.'

'And you think that means *not* IRA?'

'I'm quite sure. The krauts are quite happy for the IRA to make a nuisance of themselves but they aren't going to arm them with plastic explosives, and the latest types of fuses and detonators. There's not enough to go around for the Wehrmacht and the specialists let alone outsiders.'

'So if it wasn't IRA, who was it?'

Hastings shrugged, but amiably. 'I guess that's for you guys to sort out.'

Then the tea came in and they waited until the girl had gone.

Hastings said, 'I'd say you've got a group of pro-Germans acting on orders or they've sent some sort of raiding party over.'

'How many d'you reckon?'

'At least four, but it could be more.'

'What kind of group would you bet on?'

'I'd have thought pro-German English myself.'

'Why?'

'Whoever they are they know their way around. And they're sure of themselves.'

'Has a report gone in to Joint Intelligence on this?'

'Yes. But it's a report only. No speculation. That's your people's business.'

'Thanks for the help.' Phillips stood up.

'Does the majority mean you're moving on?'

'No. Just a new establishment. Same old job.'

They had finished their evening meal. Schultz had not joined them, and von Bayer and Ushi Lange were going up to prepare for the evening transmission. There was nothing to report but he was interested in checking what Kästner's reaction was to their success. Although Kästner might not have had a chance to check out the latest results. The Luftwaffe might not have photographed the area that day. Or Kästner might have no easy access.

As he stood at the foot of the stairs von Bayer turned to look at Rudi Kruger.

'Any idea where Otto Schultz is. Is he in his room?'

'No, Herr Sturmbannführer. He went out at midday. Said he wanted some fresh air.'

'Tell him I want to see him before he turns in.'

'Yes sir.'

Ushi had given the call-sign three times before Kästner acknowledged. But when his return message was decoded it was obvious that the Luftwaffe had already checked, and that Kästner was delighted with the results.

It had been a squadron of Messerschmitt Bf-110s from Erprobungsgruppe 210 that had photographed the airfield at Hawkinge on their way to a quick check on Biggin Hill.

Apart from the Intelligence Officer attached to squadrons

and responsible for briefing and debriefing, the Luftwaffe had its own intelligence service directly under the command of Reichsmarschall Goering.

Leutnant Falk, the I.O. stationed at Calais, had twice debriefed pilots from photographic sorties whose photographs had shown extensive damage at enemy installations that were in the beaten zone of II Fliegerkorps HQ at Ghent, but had not been targets for sorties from his HQ.

He didn't speculate on the reasons, but nevertheless suspected that maybe IX Flieger division at Soesterberg in Holland might be taking advantage of its nearness to the English south coast and indulging in a little free-lance operating. It was no skin off Leutnant Falk's nose but it could be if he didn't report it back to his HQ at Ghent. He had included a set of photographs from the reconnaissance at the radar station at Rye and the fighter airfield at Hawkinge.

In Leutnant Falk's guidebook there were crossed-keys against the entry for *Le Sauvage* in the Rue Royale in Calais. And on the first inside page against crossed keys it said – '*Confortable avec chambres de grand confort.*' And although in his humble way he respected French cuisine his mind was more on the *chambres de grand confort*. It was one of those that he had booked for his two days' leave. Previously he had spent his short leaves cycling around the nearby countryside, venturing as far as St Omer or Desvres. His long leaves he spent, of course, in Goslar with his wife and children.

The reason for the *chambres de grand confort* worked in the *pharmacie* in the Rue Royale and she was eighteen. Leutnant Falk was forty-seven next birthday and there had already been talk of an honourable discharge from the Luftwaffe. At the moment he was not pressing the point. One of the fighter pilots had shown him a photograph of the girl, naked, with her legs invitingly spread as she smiled at the camera. She was very pretty and Leutnant Falk had said the photograph made him think of Beethoven's Pastoral Symphony. The fighter pilot said it made him think she was a pretty, young whore. Which, of course, she was. Leutnant Falk, being a trained intelligence officer, had weaselled out

138

from the fighter pilot the girl's name and the address where he usually contacted her.

He had waited one evening in August, outside the shop, a bunch of flowers clutched in his hand. He had accosted her diffidently in his halting French and had been slightly nonplussed by her response. In fluent German she had told him the price and suggested where they could do it. It looked like much the same field that had been the background in the photograph. He saw her twice a week and when it rained they did it in his car. But this night it was going to be a splendid meal and then *une chambre de grand confort*.

The waiters had been insolent and slow, but then they always were, it was their pathetic way of retaliating for having lost the war. And Falk looked across the table at the pretty girl, the gold swastika on the gold chain that he had given her, nestling between her gorgeous half-naked breasts. Falk found that he hadn't much of an appetite but the girl ploughed solidly through every course, and he was actually paying the bill when Feldwebel Gross plunged into the restaurant, hat in hand.

'It's Brussels, Herr Leutnant. You are to telephone them: Oberst Schumacher, immediately. From the base, he said, not outside.'

'When did he call?'

'Twenty minutes ago, Herr Leutnant. He will be waiting for your call.'

He escorted Danielle to the room he had booked and told her that he would be back within the hour.

Back at the base he had put through the call to Oberst Schumacher at HQ Luftflotte 2, whose voice was rasping and authoritative, and who sounded in a bad mood.

'The reports you sent through to Ghent, Herr Leutnant. Who authorized the photography?'

'I don't know, Herr Oberst.'

'For God's sake, Falk, you brief the pilots don't you?'

'Yes, Herr Oberst.'

'So who initiated the sorties?'

'I don't know, Herr Oberst. I don't brief them.'

'Are they not on the war diary sheets?'

'No, Herr Oberst. They're not on our records.'

'Tell Oberst-leutnant Schraft to come to the phone.'

'Yes, Herr Oberst.'

Five minutes later Falk was back with the news. Oberst-leutnant Schraft was somewhere over England escorting a flock of Dorniers on a night raid on London. The message from Brussels was that Oberst-leutnant Schraft was to phone Oberst Schumacher as soon as he landed. Before being de-briefed.

Two hours later a tired and irritable Schraft unwound his silk scarf from around his neck and wiped his eyes.

'What does *that* bastard want at this time of night?'

Falk explained and Schraft looked at him.

'You stupid little bastard.'

Oberst-leutnant Schraft wore a Knight's Cross with swords and diamonds and he didn't give a damn for Schumacher but an order was an order, so he phoned. He smoked as he listened to Schumacher's tirade, and when there was a suitable silence at the other end he said, 'Don't get so worked up my friend. The Erprobungsgruppe were testing re-serviced engines both times. I was asked to have a look at the two sites and it's as well we did.'

'You say you were asked. Who asked you?'

'A friend of mine. An Abwehr officer.'

'Since when have the Abwehr been giving orders to the Luftwaffe may I ask.'

'I said *asked* me, not ordered me. What the hell does it matter. The squadron had to go somewhere.'

'Who was the Abwehr officer? I demand to know.'

'Don't bloody well shout at me, Schumacher. I've just come back from London while you've been sitting on your arse in Brussels.'

'Who was the Abwehr officer, Schraft, or I'll have you grounded?'

'His name is Kästner and you couldn't have me grounded if you tried till Christmas, you pig's arse.'

And Oberst-leutnant Schraft hung-up. Safe in the knowledge that what he had said was fact. He was one rank down from Schumacher but only for another two weeks.

Fourteen

Kästner had gone to his office each day despite his leave. It gave him access to information and it kept his mind off von Bayer and his gang. On this particular morning he had the feeling that it could be just the right time to make von Bayer's team official. Another couple of weeks and they would have to be pulled out. Thank God they had done so well. God knows how he would have got them back if they had failed.

There was a brief note on his desk. Typed. It said – 'Report to the Admiral immediately.'

He had thought that Admiral Canaris, head of the Abwehr, was in Spain offering Franco Gibraltar in return for a token participation on the Axis side.

He walked down the long corridor to the Admiral's secretariat, straightening his tie as he went. He sensed an odd look in the secretary's eye as he announced him on the intercom. The secretary hung up.

'Go right in, Herr Oberst.'

The Admiral was gazing out of the windows and he didn't turn as Kästner stood there.

'Sit down, Kästner.'

Then the old man turned, and sat down at the other side of his big, old-fashioned desk.

'I've had a complaint, Kästner. I'm told you've been giving orders to Luftwaffe units. What's it all about?'

'I've never given orders to any Luftwaffe unit, sir. But I did ask if it was possible for a photo-reconnaissance to be done in two particular areas.'

'Why?'

'I wanted to check if they had been damaged.'

'So why not a routine check through normal channels?'

'I needed to know quickly.'

'Why? I thought you were on leave from Sea-Lion.'

'I am, sir.'

'So why did you want to know?'

Kästner hesitated for a moment and then decided that this was the moment to make von Bayer a hero. For fifteen minutes Canaris listened and questioned him. Even at the end he seemed full of disbelief.

'How did he recruit these men?'

'Just talked to them. Told them what had to be done.'

'Have you records of the signals traffic between you?'

'Yes, sir.'

'How did they get over there?'

'By U-boat.'

'Good God Almighty. Who authorized *that*?'

'Nobody, sir.'

'I find this incredible, Kästner. You must be out of your mind.'

'They've done what they set out to do.'

Canaris closed his eyes. When he opened them he lifted the phone.

'Get me Reichsmarschall Goering. He's at Karinhall.'

He sat waiting with the phone to his ear. It was two or three minutes before he spoke. Choosing his words carefully and diplomatically he told Goering of the complaint from Luftflotte 2 and most of the details of von Bayer and his team. When he had finished he waited. Even from where he sat Kästner could hear the Reichsmarschall's roar. But it was a roar of laughter, and as his voice boomed on, Canaris relaxed. Finally he said, 'I shall be much obliged, Herr Reichsmarschall.'

He put the phone down slowly and carefully to give himself time to sort out his words. When he looked at Kästner he said, 'God must be on your side, Kästner. Goering was delighted. Said he wished we had more like von Bayer. And said if he wasn't so busy he would go over and fly them back himself. He is going to inform the Führer immediately.' He shook his head slowly. 'All the same you were a fool, Kästner. Irresponsible. You'd better hang around here until I get more news.'

Kästner sat at his desk trying to concentrate on the report that outlined what the Abwehr's responsibilities would be after Week Two of 'Operation Barbarossa', the attack on Russia.

He was putting on his hat and coat to go for lunch when the two men came into his office. They both wore Gestapo uniforms. The tall one said, 'Kästner?'

'Yes, I'm Oberst Kästner.'

The other man moved over to him, patting his body to check if he had a weapon.

'What's going on?'

'You're under arrest.'

'Can I see your warrant?'

Kästner's hand reached for the telephone, and then noticed the Walther pistol in the taller one's hand.

'Don't make a fuss, Kästner. Just do what you're told.'

'I need to tell my superiors.'

'They know already.'

'Where are you taking me?'

'To the Albrechtstrasse.'

Kästner walked with them down the back stairs to where a car was waiting in the courtyard at the back of the building. There was a uniformed driver and he was pushed into the back seat between the two Gestapo men.

At Gestapo headquarters he walked slowly up the wide steps of the main entrance and then he was escorted across the big hall to the wide staircase. Their heel clicks echoed on the tiled floor as they walked with him to the far end of the first floor. They turned down a long corridor and half-way down they stopped at a big door that held a small board with gold lettering. It said 'Geheimrat Lemke Amt V'.

The tall man knocked on the door, a voice called out and the Gestapo man opened the door and waved Kästner inside. A man in his early fifties got up from behind his desk. He was balding, with a pale scholarly face. He waved to the two armchairs in the corner of the room. He nodded to the Gestapo man to leave and then held out his soft hand to Kästner.

'Oberst Kästner, I believe. Geheimrat Lemke. Do sit down. There is no need for formality.'

When they were both seated Lemke said, 'You will know, of course, why you are here.'

'I'm afraid I don't.'

The Geheimrat smiled a patient, experienced smile, and his soft voice was almost like a woman's.

'So often our interviews start with those words. Let me explain. You are under arrest on a warrant, signed personally by the Reichsführer der SS Heinrich Himmler. He initiated this action on the personal instructions of the Führer himself. I understand that this was after certain information had been laid before him by Reichsmarschall Goering. Is that clear?'

'What am I accused of?'

'High treason, Herr Oberst.'

'But Goering told Admiral Canaris that he was delighted. I was there when they spoke on the telephone.'

'So you *do* know what I am talking about?'

'Not in terms of high treason. The opposite. Excessive loyalty, maybe.'

Geheimrat Lemke smiled. A contented cat's smile.

'It always surprises people when they learn how the law interprets their actions. In your case the charges, even at this early stage, are on over fifty separate counts. So you will understand my concern.'

Kästner shrugged. 'I think you will find this is a big mistake.'

Lemke smiled. 'I wish I had just one Reichsmark for every time I have heard those words, Herr Oberst. I should be a rich man.'

'Are you Gestapo, Herr Geheimrat?'

'Oh yes. In a legal capacity only, you understand.'

'Am I allowed to call a lawyer?'

'Who is your lawyer, Herr Oberst?'

Kästner sighed. 'Never mind. I don't need a lawyer. What is it you want to know?'

'That's very simple. I want to know everything. Names, dates, and everything that has happened, so far. Particularly I want to know when you are next due to communicate with these people.'

'I should want to know first if similar charges will be brought against them.'

'Of course. They too are traitors.'

'They are brave men, for God's sake. They are risking their lives for Germany.'

'I'm afraid that that is not the view of the authorities, Herr Oberst.'

'And you expect me to betray them?'

'I expect you to co-operate in any manner required of you by your Commander-in-Chief to whom you have sworn an oath of loyalty. I have your signed copy in your file on my desk. Perhaps I can remind you of the words.' Lemke coughed before he read from the paper. 'I swear by God this holy oath, to obey without question the leader of the German people and supreme commander of the German forces, Adolf Hitler. And to serve him as a brave soldier, ready, on this oath to lay down his life.' He paused. 'You remember that, Herr Oberst? You signed it on 4 August 1937.'

Kästner nodded but didn't speak. He could see the net closing round them all.

Fifteen

There had been no response from Kästner when they went on network at nine. And there was no response at ten.

It was after that attempt at contact that von Bayer heard the shouting. At the bottom of the stairs Schultz was sprawled on his back. Rudi Kruger and Erich Voss stood looking down at him.

'What's going on?' von Bayer asked.

'He's passed out. He's drunk.'

'Where did he get the drink?' Von Bayer looked from Voss to Kruger who looked embarrassed and uneasy.

'Where did he get the drink, Rudi?'

'I'm not sure, Herr Sturmbannführer.'

'Where do you think he got it, for God's sake?'

Kruger looked at Voss, who hesitated for a moment and then walked away a few paces and signalled to von Bayer to join him. He spoke almost in a whisper.

'I think we've got trouble, Max. Schultz came in ten minutes ago, shouting and cursing. He was obviously drunk. We think he's been on the rampage. He told Rudi yesterday that he wanted a woman. There's blood on his trousers and scratches on his arms and neck. I'd say that he got the drink before he raped some woman.'

'You and Rudi carry him into the big barn. I'll be with you in a couple of minutes.'

As von Bayer walked up the stairs to his bedroom he knew that he had to stop the rot. He couldn't think how it had happened, or what had caused it, but with that instinct that

146

good leaders have, he knew that in some way the tide was turning against them.

They had obviously been trying to bring Schultz round. A bucket of water was alongside him and the front of his shirt was wet. His eyes were opening and closing slowly, and his big chest was heaving. Von Bayer's hands tore at the buttons on Schultz's flies and pulled up his shirt. There was blood around his genitals and on the insides of his thighs. His hand went out to grasp Schultz's curly hair, shaking his head violently.

'Where've you been, Schultz? Tell me.'

Schultz opened his eyes and tried to focus on von Bayer's face.

'Who that?' he muttered.

'It's me, von Bayer. Where have you been?'

Schultz shook his head slowly and von Bayer cursed slowly and stood up. He reached for the bucket of water and emptied it over Schultz's head. Schultz struggled until he was sitting up, his hair plastered down on his skull, his eyes red-rimmed as he looked at von Bayer.

'What's all that for, you . . .'

Then von Bayer was straddling Schultz's body, kneeling so that his face was close to Schultz's face.

'Where have you been, Schultz? Tell me.'

'What's it to do with you mister. I'm not one of your bloody SS men.'

Then the tip of von Bayer's pistol was touching Schultz's face. Cold and hard. Schultz tried to lift an arm to brush it away but he couldn't move.

'Tell me, Schultz. Everything. Or I'll blow your head off.'

Schultz belched and there was vomit at the corner of his mouth. He heard the click as the safety catch came off.

'On bicycle. She was on a bicycle. Took her in the woods. Had to do it when she was shouting and screaming.'

'You raped her.'

'You could have had her too. All of you. Fantastic.'

'And then you killed her.'

'Yes. Too much noise.'

'Where's her body?'

Schultz grinned. 'They won't find it for months.'

'Where is she?'

His head rolled to one side and his eyes closed, 'God knows.'

Only Voss realized what was going to happen and he held his breath as he saw von Bayer's finger squeeze the trigger.

Voss helped Kruger dig the hole in the barn floor where they buried Schultz's body and then put the bales of straw back over the disturbed soil. But they did it in silence.

Geheimrat Lemke had planned one of his subtle interrogations for Kästner. They always worked with the intelligent ones. The touch of sympathy, a hint of actual approval, the long chats, and the pieces would fall into place. A week to ten days would be enough. But it was not to be. Schellenberg had called him to his office. If he couldn't get it out of Kästner that evening they would give him the treatment. Who were the men involved, and where were they? That's what they wanted to know, and Schellenberg made clear that the pressure came right from the top. He, Schellenberg, was being asked for hourly reports by the Führer and he wanted something to report every hour.

Lemke had had to deal with these kinds of situations before. He had to admit that their crudity speeded things up but he wasn't sure that they always got the right information. But for him it certainly clarified the situation. The decision would have to be Kästner's.

He switched on an extra light as he walked into his office and nodded to the guard to go. Then he sat down in his comfortable leather chair, looking towards the window as he assembled the words.

'How do you withstand physical pain, Herr Oberst? Would it be a problem?'

'I don't understand.'

Geheimrat Lemke looked at his watch. 'I've been given two hours to get the full information from you. There are strict orders that it must be available by ten o'clock this evening. They have allowed me one hour to convince you that you should talk to me in a civilized fashion, after that

I'm afraid it would be in other hands. So what do we do?'

'What will happen to these people if I give you the information?'

'I don't really know. I seldom do. But in this particular case I don't think even Schellenberg knows what it's all about. When the Reichsführer wants information we hasten to supply it. *How* it gets used is not our problem.'

'How much is known already?'

'Almost nothing I'm afraid. Nothing but what you told Canaris and he passed on to Goering. And which Goering passed on to the Führer. And now the music has stopped and I'm holding the parcel. You.'

Kästner sat silently. Trying to think. But it wasn't possible. And Lemke spoke again.

'Can I make a suggestion, Herr Oberst?'

'Of course.'

'Almost everybody talks under physical pressure. And most people talk when the first pain is felt. Until then they have no idea of what the pain would be like. If you would find it helpful I will arrange for you to experience that first stage of pressure. Then perhaps we could talk again.'

Kästner looked at Geheimrat Lemke. He had taken the point.

'I'm not a hero, Geheimrat Lemke, and I am convinced that these people have done no wrong.'

'A wise piece of thinking if I may say so. Who knows, they may all end up with Knight's Crosses. Now. Let's take it slowly.'

Despite the urgency and the pressure, a whole day had been lost because the Führer had gone down to Berchtesgaden for a few days and Schellenberg had had to take down the report himself.

Walter Schellenberg was an energetic man who had made his reputation with the capture of two important British Intelligence offcers at Venlo in the first days of the war. Their capture was due more to their naïveté than Schellenberg's skill, but it had provided German Intelligence with British secret codes and a list of most of SIS's links in Holland and Czechoslovakia. And the timing was right.

As head of the RSHA, Schellenberg was answerable directly to the Reichsführer der SS Heinrich Himmler, who reported directly to the Führer himself. And whilst Himmler was not an ideal companion for a long journey, Schellenberg preferred Himmler's presence when he had to have his infrequent interviews with the Führer. There was something about Adolf Hitler that made Schellenberg uneasy when he was the sole target for those penetrating eyes. Hitler seemed to know things that nobody could have told him. Like women, he could sense an atmosphere. Somebody had once said that Adolf Hitler was like Joan of Arc. He heard voices telling him what to do.

There was a log fire burning in the big room, casting its glow on the honey-coloured wooden floor. It was a cosy room, not glaringly ornate. There were plenty of businessmen with far more elaborate retreats than this.

His report had been taken to the Führer by one of his aides and Schellenberg sat patiently, waiting to be called. For once in his career he had no idea how his information would be received. With praise or vilification.

The Führer came in himself after Schellenberg had waited for two hours. There were no greetings and no comments. Just a stream of instructions.

Kästner would be used to keep contact with the rebels. The British would be informed through Stockholm of their presence and the Luftwaffe would supply an aircraft to pick them up. There would be full co-operation with London to stop any further acts by the group. When they were back on German soil they would be arrested. A daily report would be submitted to the Führer wherever he might be. The matter was top secret and top priority.

They had Heil-Hitlered, and Schellenberg had left.

The two men sat with Kästner in his study at his flat, watching closely as he tapped out his message to von Bayer. And in England von Bayer breathed a sigh of relief that they were in contact again after two days' silence.

But he was surprised at the message. It seemed that Kästner had told the authorities, who were pleased at what had been achieved. However, for their own safety, the operation should cease immediately and arrangements would be made to get them out.

In Stockholm as in Lisbon, the lights had never gone out, but there was a vast difference between the two capitals. In Lisbon the espionage war and the war of diplomacy were hard-edged and ruthless. The neutrality of Stockholm was different, a friendlier neutrality that came from a self-assurance that allowed her to trade vital iron-ore to Germany while her general public openly sympathized with the British.

There were aristocracies in Sweden, Germany and England, that had inter-married and entertained one another for too long for their relationship to change merely because of a war. Uncles and aunts, cousins and nephews, didn't suddenly become mortal enemies just because the Nazis would like it that way. They were loyal to their respective countries and if Cousin Willi in Berlin was in the Abwehr, or Uncle Henry in London puffed up the steps of the War Office, that was how it had to be until this ghastly war was over. Except on the British side, nobody prayed that Hitler would lose, but neither did anyone hope that he would win. The war was like some grinding internal pain, to be ignored in the hope that it would go away. The *Almanach de Gotha* and *Burke's Peerage* were more significant than either side's *War Bulletins*.

It was not considered odd in Stockholm for the old King to have an Englishman as his tennis partner against the two young Germans from their embassy. The King was much-loved, and he and his partner were always allowed to win. He was a good tennis player anyway, and when they assembled later for their lemonade or gin there were helpful things that could be said across the frontiers that would have been embarrassing or dangerous, even in a diplomatic bag.

It was in the changing-room that Freiherr von Edel had passed the word to His Majesty's Ambassador to Sweden and had suggested that the military attachés of the British and German embassies might meet later that day at the old church at Skansen.

The two emissaries duly met, and as they watched the children and their pretty mothers, Oberst-leutnant Bergman passed on his news to Lieutenant-Colonel Villiers.

'Why the hell are you telling me this, Theo?'

'I've had orders to tell you. As I said, they were not authorized to do this. They're an embarrassment.'

'And you want them back sound in wind and limb.'

'Look at that girl, the blonde with the pram, imagine coming home to that every night.'

'She's one of yours, dear boy. A kraut not a Swede. And it's not her baby. She's nursemaid to Signora Bertoli whose husband is commercial attaché at the Italian embassy. Rumour says she screws like a rattle-snake.'

'Propaganda, dear boy, she's a clean-limbed member of the BDM or she wouldn't be here. All the same, I wish she wouldn't keep bending over that pram. What were you saying?'

'And you want your chaps back in one piece?'

Oberst-leutnant Bergman looked at his companion.

'I don't remember saying that, old man.'

'Where are they?'

'Now that's the problem. We don't know. It's a bit like the BBC news bulletins when the Luftwaffe lays its eggs. You always say "somewhere in south-east England". And that's about all we can say.'

'Have you got names and descriptions?'

'Better than that. I've got names, descriptions and photographs.'

'Are you handing those over?'

'In due course, my friend. When you've chatted to London and you've got a reaction, then I'm sure we'll co-operate. That's why I'm here right now.'

'London could well be a bit touchy if they've done the things you've told me.'

'They could well be. All we ask is that you don't make a song and dance about it.'

'In what way?'

'Putting them on trial. That sort of thing.'

'But they've killed people, for God's sake.'

'OK, shoot them, but don't make a pantomime of it.'

'And then we'll have Goebbels or Ribbentrop shouting about the Geneva Convention.'

'These people aren't covered by the Geneva Convention.'

'I'll pass the word to London and let you know what they say.'

The message back from London was uncompromising and forthright. If they were given all details of the 'irregulars', and assistance in locating them, then they would be taken prisoner and interned. They would be tried for any crimes they might have committed against personnel. Damage to installations not involving death or injury would be ignored. The only concession was that they agreed to there being no publicity. A separate signal had instructed Lt-Col Villiers to try to find out why the Germans were so anxious to avoid publicity.

Villiers had met Bergman in the Maritime Museum. The German had listened impassively as Villiers passed on London's message. When it was finished Bergman sighed.

'As always, London has to look the gift horse in the mouth.'

'Just checking that it is a horse, Theo.'

'How the hell are we going to locate them? Tell me that.'

'You can suggest some RV where you'll pick them up.'

Bergman sighed again. He was a soldier and this wasn't soldiers' stuff. He looked up at Villiers' face.

'They really are shits, aren't they?'

'Who?'

'Your lot and my lot. Neither of them give a damn about these people. They're brave by anybody's standards, but they've done something without being ordered to do it. So they're fair game to be hunted down.'

'Why are your people so keen on hushing it up?'

'God knows. I've tried to puzzle it out. But it doesn't make sense. Our public would love it if they heard about it.'

'Ours not to reason why, Theo. Anyway, is it a deal?'

153

'Yes. The stuff's in my guidebook. I'll hand it to you as I go.'

He looked at Villiers' face intently. 'Don't let your bastards crucify them, Joe.'

'I'll do what I can.'

Bergman handed over the guidebook and headed for the exit, mentally writing an application to be returned to his unit. It was dark and foggy outside. Stockholm in November matched his mood. But he would have to pass on the details of the deal to Berlin so that the bastards could bait the trap for their own people.

Sixteen

Von Bayer and Kleist sat in von Bayer's bedroom, reading and re-reading the last message that had come from Kästner at the nine o'clock call that evening. There were congratulations all round again and they were requested to give a map reference of their location.

'I feel there's something going wrong, Walter. I told Kästner that I would never give a location.'

'Why, Max?'

'It would be crazy. Our code wouldn't fool a schoolboy and if the British put a DF unit on us they'd trace us in a couple of hours in an isolated place like this. But if we gave a map reference they would be here in ten minutes. Kästner knows this and still suggests it.'

'What do you think is wrong?'

'I just don't know, Walter. It may be nothing to do with this message. I just feel my luck's run out.'

'We've had two very successful operations, it's just reaction setting in.'

'I nearly did a really crazy thing today when I was in Cranbrook.'

Kleist smiled. 'Tell me.'

'I went into the post-office and checked with the telephone operator a telephone number in Cambridge of someone I knew. And I damn near phoned.'

'Is this the girl you told Ushi about?'

'Yes. I find she haunts me. I think about her every day. It's like a wound. It's beginning to be part of my feeling that everything's gone sour.'

'What happened. Did she turn you down?'

'No. But her old man did. They're Jewish.'

'Maybe when it's all over you can straighten it out. Did she love you?'

'I think so. She was very young. But I loved her. I still do. I had a vague feeling that coming over here would help, but it doesn't. I feel that if she'd married me I wouldn't be sitting in this dump.'

'Did the Schultz thing worry you?'

'Not really. It had to be done. It was just one more weight. Kästner warned me that he'd be a problem.'

'What was her name? The girl.'

'Sadie. Sadie Aarons, and she was so gentle, and so beautiful.'

Kleist raised his glass of milk. 'To you and Sadie Aarons. May it all come right.'

Kleist struggled awkwardly to his feet.

'Go to bed, Max. Rest.'

The next evening von Bayer sat with Ushi Lange as she rigged up the radio. His own message was a brief acknowledgement of the previous day's signal from Kästner.

He watched her tap it out and switch to receive, the pad and pencil ready in her hand. As the needle started to flicker he saw her frown and her pencil was racing over the paper. Page after page. It took no more than ten minutes but he could see the perspiration on her forehead and the stern set of her mouth as she took down the Morse. Then the needle was at zero and Ushi leaned forward to switch off the power.

She leaned back and lifted the headphones off her ears, shaking her head to settle her hair. She turned to look at him, her face pale.

'It wasn't Kästner. It was a signals operator and the message is from the OKW.'

He reached for the pad in disbelief. The OKW was the Oberkommando der Wehrmacht. The German General Staff. The message was in clear and in German.

'OKW SIGNAL 97431 TO VON BAYER STOP YOU WILL CEASE ALL OPERATIONS ON RECEIPT THIS SIGNAL STOP YOU WILL ACKNOWLEDGE RECEIPT NEXT TRANSMISSION AND CONFIRM YOUR STATUS STOP YOU WILL TRANSMIT YOUR LOCATION BY MAP REFERENCE USING ORDNANCE SURVEY DATA STOP YOU WILL REMAIN AT PRESENT LOCATION STOP YOUR FATHER AND KASTNER REPEAT KASTNER ARE AT PRESENT IN CUSTODY STOP FAILURE TO CARRY OUT THESE ORDERS WILL LEAD TO ACTION AGAINST THEM STOP SIGNATURE OBERST-GENERAL STADLER OKW MESSAGE ENDS'

There was an eerie silence everywhere, as if the world had suddenly stopped, and he closed his eyes as the room swung sickeningly.

It was Voss who spotted the car coming slowly up the drive and they carried out their usual drill. Only the English speakers stayed in the house, and now it was only Kruger who had to make himself scarce at the top of the barn.

The two men who got out of the car seemed in no great hurry to come to the door, they stood looking around the general area, one of them stretching out his arms and pointing towards the back of the house. They both wore dark blue raincoats and brown trilby hats. Both men were about the same height, one tall and thin, the other tall and more solidly built.

Eventually they turned and walked up the path and knocked on the door. Von Bayer opened it and the thin man said. 'Good-morning, sir. We're from the police and we're making some inquiries. We'd like a word with you if it's convenient.' And he held out his warrant for von Bayer to inspect.

'Do come in.'

'Thank you, sir.'

Von Bayer led them into the drawing-room and waved them to the armchairs. The thin one said, 'My name's Carter. Detective Inspector Carter, and my colleague here is Detective Sergeant Oakes from Cranbrook.'

As he spoke Carter took off his raincoat before he sat

down. As he was sitting down he said, 'I expect you heard about the tragedy, sir.'

'I'm afraid I haven't.'

'A young girl, sir. Murdered and sexually assaulted. A nasty business.'

'You mean a local girl.'

'Yes. You might have seen her around. Worked at the baker's in Cranbrook. A dark-haired girl. Eighteen years old. A pretty young thing.'

'When did this happen?'

'A few days ago.'

'I don't think I've seen her about. But my girlfriend does most of the shopping.'

'We'll have a word with her later.'

'Certainly.'

'The body was only discovered yesterday, there'll be a post-mortem of course.' He leaned back in his chair. 'How long have you been living here, sir?'

'About two weeks.'

'Have you seen any strangers about in that time. Gipsies, tramps, hawkers, anything like that?'

'Not that I can recall. But we're a bit off the beaten track here for passers-by.'

'Of course. Several people mention seeing a chap on the outskirts of Cranbrook. Tough-looking fellow. Black curly hair, solidly built. Two of our informants said he looked the worse for drink. He was shouting, and they reckon he was speaking German. It could be some other language of course, neither of our informants actually speaks German. You've not seen anyone about answering to that description?'

Von Bayer smiled. 'If I had I think I'd have been along to the police station. He sounds pretty wild.'

'He may be nothing to do with this affair of course. We have to pursue every lead, but whoever did this is a very dangerous man. A sick man who'll probably do it again. Where were you living before you came here, sir?'

'In Cambridge.'

Carter turned to the Det. Sergeant. 'Your notebook, George,' then he turned back to von Bayer. 'Your name, sir?'

'Barnes. Max Barnes.'

'And your old address?'

'37 St John's Road.'

'Have you got your identity card handy?'

'Yes.'

Von Bayer fished in his inside pocket and handed the card to Carter who looked at it carefully and then handed it back.

'I'd like to see your young lady if I may.'

'Of course. I'll find her.'

Ushi had not been told any details about Schultz so her surprise at the news was genuine. The Inspector was heavily gallant, and it was over in five minutes. They accepted the offer of tea and seemed in no hurry to go.

'Is there anyone else living here or staying here at the moment?'

'Yes there are two friends of ours.'

'Men?'

'Yes.'

'Ah well, I'd better have a word with them.'

'D'you want to see them separately?'

'No. I just want George to have their details.'

Voss was completely relaxed and played the returned White Hunter with all the conviction that the truth provides.

'You must have had a very interesting life, Mr Vernon.'

'It's just a job, Inspector, much the same as yours. As time goes by the shine wears off.'

'Quite so.'

Walter Kleist was quiet but co-operative and neither of them was anything like the suspect. The policemen both seemed perfectly relaxed as they walked to the door.

Standing for a moment on the door-step looking out across the yard Carter turned to von Bayer. 'By the way, Mr Barnes. I never asked you what you're doing down here?'

'I'm hoping to start a small stables. Breaking and schooling horses and that sort of thing. But there are a lot of problems.'

'What sort of problems?'

'The difficulty of getting feed, and the land here is already rented out.'

'Well, we'll be getting on our way. Thanks for your time.'

He raised his hat, and the two of them walked slowly over to the car.

As they drove back towards Cranbrook Carter lit a cigarette.

'Well. What did you think of 'em, George?'

'I don't see any of them beating up young girls. Not raping either.'

'What makes you say that?'

'Well the older one, Vernon, isn't strong enough. And the other two, Barnes and Gorst, don't need to rape. They're well off and plenty of charm, they'd get what they wanted without raping for it. I'd think Gorst, the one with the big brown eyes, could be a homo.'

'You never know, George. Psychos don't just do it for a screw. The beating up and the killing's all part of their satisfaction.'

As they pulled into the police-station yard Carter said, 'All the same, check those addresses, George.'

'OK, guv'nor.'

'We've got to get out of here, Walter. And fast. When they check those addresses they'll be back.'

'I'm afraid you're right, Max. Can you let Kästner know?'

Von Bayer told Kleist about the signal from the OKW.

'Have you acknowledged it, Max?'

'No. I didn't last night, anyway.'

'Why not?'

'I don't know. Instinct, I suppose. It doesn't hang together. First the congratulations and now this.'

'How the hell do we get back without help from Berlin?'

'I'm not sure how but I'm sure we can.'

'Where are we going right now?'

'There's a village down the road called Hawkhurst. We'll go there tonight. We've got to stay inside the Defence Area or we'll be challenged for passes and we haven't got them.'

Major Phillips was not too pleased at being brought back into SIS's headquarters at Broadway just opposite St James's Park tube station. Life on detachment was much more civilized, and the Broadway building had all the dreariness of a Victorian poor-house. Even inside, the offices were gloomy and cramped from the influx of new experts. And it was going to take him months to catch up with the office politics. With so many of its alumni, like himself, the products of Eton and Oxbridge or Lincoln's Inn, and the gloomy building itself, he sometimes wondered why they didn't have a fagging system and a head boy. And all the dim ex-Indian Police chaps were really the end.

It was only because he had been concerned with the sabotage at the Rye radar station that he was stuck with his present little jig-saw puzzle. He had laid out all the bits and pieces on the trestle table.

There were his own reports on the attacks at Rye and Hawkinge. A sheaf of monitored radio traffic from Signals Security covering sixteen two-way contacts. These had been sent to the GCCS at Bletchley and their report was pinned to the monitored stuff. He wondered whether the report from GCCS was a dig at SIS or a serious comment. They had pointed out that the messages were a simple one letter shift code, and apologized for the seventy-two hour delay, as they assumed that SIS suspected a secondary concealed code and had spent time investigating the possibility. They concluded, however, that as the messages made sense and were in simple German and that no block system had been used, they were simply what they appeared to be, and suggested that a couple of DF vans would solve the problem. A sensible idea, except that there had been no transmissions for two nights, and nobody had any idea of the transmitter's location. There were the detonator caps in two cardboard boxes; the Irish passport; a report on a meeting between the two military attachés in Stockholm; and the list of names and photographs of the suspected saboteurs.

He had asked for a Foreign Office and War Office appreciation of why the German General Staff were selling their people down the river and had received a tart order to get on with his investigation. And that, he reckoned, meant that the bastards didn't know.

For the hundredth time he looked at the Ordnance Survey map where he had ringed the sites at Rye and Hawkinge. He lay the ruler between them and drew a straight line. So where would you conveniently stake out to cover these two places? Lacking inspiration he drew an equal-sided triangle using this line as its base. This was the obvious area but if they were as bright as they seemed to be then this was probably the area they avoided. He sighed and threw down his pencil. He looked at the photographs of the Germans. There were only five although the list had given the name of a girl. They were the usual random snapshots that had been gathered together in a hurry. There were captions on the back of some of them. There was a man in a bush jacket squinting into the sun, a rifle with a telescopic sight under one arm. Beside him a huge hairy man, bare-chested and sweaty looking, with his foot on the head of a long lean lion. A pretty, middle-aged, blonde woman looked up at him fondly. He turned over the photograph. The caption read. 'Erich Voss. Nairobi 1938 with American author Hemingway.' There was a photograph of a handsome young man on a horse, leaning forward in the saddle to take a silver salver. The caption said: 'Maximilian von Bayer, only son of Baron Ludwig von Bayer. Receiving first prize Erfurt 1937.'

Von Bayer wrapped the yellow oilskin carefully round the documents and slid on the wide elastic band. Everything personal that he was going to take with him was in the package.

He walked down to the yard and watched Voss and Kruger loading the guns and ammunition into the boot of the car. The tins of food and the thermos were on the ground waiting to go in last. He put the binoculars and one compass on the front seat of the car. When the boot had been loaded he put two of the canvas sheets from the barn to cover the stuff before he closed the lid.

Slowly he walked over to the hole that had been dug at the side of the small barn. The last bundles of gelignite. The boxes of detonators. The radio. One of Voss's rifles. Two suitcases packed with personal things. He had insisted that they must travel light with only bare essentials. He reached for the spade and slowly filled in the hole from the heaps of spoil. When he had trodden the surface level he put back the turves that had been cut before the hole was dug. His limbs felt heavy and he no longer had a real plan. He had in mind making for the coast to steal or capture a boat in an attempt to get across the Channel under cover of darkness. For some reason his tired mind kept going back to the abandoned farmhouse that he had had in mind as their first head-quarters when he was planning the operation in Schloss Eger. In some odd way it had become some sort of sanctuary. A kind of neutral territory.

Ushi made them a last bowl of warm soup and the five of them stood or sat in the living-room like a family waiting for the removal men. Anxious to go, but conscious of the discomforts ahead.

It was dark when they left. Von Bayer drove carefully and slowly down the narrow country lane and Kleist, sitting beside him, read the map and gave him the route as they went along.

Hawkhurst had once been the centre of the Wealden iron industry but as they drove along the main street it looked to the Germans like some deserted film-lot left over from the making of a western. The long line of white clapboard shops and houses looked eerie in the pale moonlight. Von Bayer pulled up the car against a low stone wall. As he got out he saw that it was a churchyard. The others got out of the car to stretch their legs, trying to adjust their eyes to the faint light of the moon. Rudi Kruger was the only one of them who looked cheerful.

'Ushi.'

'Yes, Max.'

'You come with me and see if we can find a place for the night.'

They crossed the deserted street and von Bayer knocked

on the first door. An elderly man came to the door. He was wearing a Home Guard uniform and he peered out at them from the darkness of the hallway.

'Who is it? I ain't eaten yet.'

'Good evening, I wonder if you could tell us where we could get a bed for the night.'

The old man called over his shoulder, 'Mother.' He turned back to look at them. 'My wife'll maybe know.'

A thin angular woman walked down the hallway, her hand smoothing along the wall to guide her.

'What is it, Edgar?'

'They want to know where they can get a bed for the night.'

'Just the two of you?' she said.

'There's five of us actually.'

She scratched her head, thinking.

'The George ain't taking anybody these days. How about Mrs Williams, Dad? She might put them up.'

'They could try,' he said.

'Where could I find Mrs Williams, ma'am?'

'D'you know Hawkhurst?'

'This is our first visit.'

'Have you got a car?'

'Yes.'

'Where's it parked?'

'Opposite, by the church.'

'They bombed it you know, those bloody Germans, went up in flames,' the old man said angrily.

'They're not interested in that, Edgar. You'll have to go back a bit, and take the road to the left down the hill. Right at the bottom, just before the turn, you'll see a house standing back from the road. On the left-hand side. Partridge House, it's called. You tell her Mrs Chapman sent you. She'll want your ration coupons if you stay more than one night.'

'Thanks for your help, Mrs Chapman.'

'That's all right.'

They clambered back into the car and turned and took the road down the hill.

Partridge House was a long, low, L-shaped building, and

from inside they could hear music. When they knocked the music stopped and it was several minutes before the door opened. The elderly lady who stood there had a red shield over the head of the torch that she shone towards the floor.

'Mrs Williams?'

'Yes.'

'Mrs Chapman suggested you might be able to give us a bed for the night.'

'How many of you are there?'

'Four men, one girl.'

'I could only do the one night.'

'That would be fine.'

Von Bayer went back to the car to tell the others and warned Kruger not to say a word. He should smile but not speak. As he took in his own kit he wondered where Mrs Williams came from. She had a slight accent. Probably Welsh, with a name like Williams.

The old lady had shown them the three rooms and left them to sort themselves out. She said she would leave the visitor's book on the hall-table for them to sign. They had to do that, she said, because of the regulations.

Rudi Kruger had stayed in his room with the door locked, with biscuits and a small tin of pressed meat.

Mrs Williams had given them poached eggs on toast and stewed apple and custard. She was a kindly soul and kept popping in and out to see that they were satisfied.

When they had finished she came in to take the debris away and she said, 'Shall I put you on a bit of music?'

'That's very kind of you, Mrs Williams.'

She wound up the small portable gramophone and put the record on carefully and turned to look at them.

'This is my favourite.'

Only Walter Kleist recognized the first few bars but as soon as it moved on the others exchanged glances. It was the waltz from *The Gipsy Princess* – '*Tausend kleine Eng'lein singen*'. And Mrs Williams softly sang the words. In German.

When it was over she smiled at them. 'It was so beautiful in those days in Vienna.'

Von Bayer smiled at her. 'Do you know Vienna, Mrs Williams?'

'Oh, Mr Barnes, I was born there. I grew up there.'

'When did you come to England?'

'The eleventh of March 1938. I won't ever forget the date.'

'Why?'

'That was the day the Nazis marched into Vienna. I'm Jewish you see. Not my husband, he was Welsh. He said we must go. Straight away. The same day. But you won't remember all that.'

Walter Kleist smiled at her. 'Shall I play you some Strauss waltzes on your piano?'

'Oh,' she said. 'I'd love that.'

Kleist limped over to the upright piano, opened the lid and dragged out the stool.

For twenty minutes he played without stopping, and the old lady sat in her pinafore, beaming, with tears trickling down her cheeks. Then Kleist turned to smile at Ushi as he played '*Ich schenk' mein Herz*'. Then he pulled down the lid and stood up.

'That was beautiful. Thank you so much.'

As he lay in his bed von Bayer wished that Sadie Aarons had been there, holding his hand as Walter played his song for him. It seemed so long ago but it was little more than two years. If they found a boat he would take the risk and telephone her before they left. He lay for a long time without sleeping and finally got out of bed. He put his coat over his shoulders and moved over to the window, pushing aside the black-out curtain.

There was frost already on the windows and the stars were sharp and bright in the dark sky. He wondered if they really would harm Kästner and his father. Surely by now they would have understood Kästner's explanations of his operation. What could they possibly object to? When he was back he would be able to sort it all out. Then there was a light knock on his door and Ushi came in.

'What is it, Ushi?'

She was crying softly as he went towards her.

'What is it?'

'It's Walter, Max. He's so ill. He made me swear I wouldn't tell you.'

'Sit down on the bed.'

He wrapped the blankets around her but she went on shivering.

'How bad is he?'

'He's in terrible pain all the time. I'm so afraid for him, Max.'

'How long has he been like this?'

'Just over a week, and there are only enough drugs left for three more days. After that it will be impossible.'

Von Bayer sat silently, his mouth dry, trying not to shiver.

'What's the name of the drug, Ushi?'

'It's opium. He's dying, Max.'

'We'll get him to a doctor, Ushi.'

'How can we do that?'

'I'll work that out, my love. Don't worry, I'll work something out for tomorrow. How is he at the moment, shall I come in and sit with him?'

'He's asleep, I gave him a double dose.'

'Try and get some sleep, Ushi. I'll get him medical help tomorrow.'

After Ushi had gone von Bayer lay on the bed in his overcoat, the blankets over his legs. If there were no road-blocks he would drive through to Ashford. There was a hospital there, he would drop Ushi Lange and her Walter, and pray that they would be treated by the British as prisoners-of-war. There was no choice. It would make little difference to Kleist. He knew already that he was going to die but Kleist would hate the fact that Ushi would be a prisoner too.

It was six o'clock in the morning when von Bayer eventually slept.

At about the same time that von Bayer went to sleep, Detective Inspector Carter and a dozen men were making their way cautiously and quietly up the drive to Cragg's Farm.

Two marksmen had given the Inspector cover with their rifles as he knocked on the solid oak door. He stood there waiting, his breath steaming in the frosty air. When there was no answer he stepped back from the porch and looked up at the bedroom windows. He told one of the men to break in through the kitchen window.

When he found that the house was empty he decided on a thorough search. By the time they had searched the house it was beginning to be light outside and he decided to go the whole hog and have the outbuildings and the grounds searched as well.

They had found the explosives and detonators first, and Carter had sent a man back to Cranbrook to notify the Special Branch officer of their find.

Long before the Special Branch officer arrived they had found Schultz's body, and a man went back to Cranbrook to notify Scotland Yard and the Murder Squad.

It was lunch-time before they found the radio and the rest of the abandoned gear and the Special Branch man phoned his masters who notified SIS.

The various holes were screened off and the pit outside the barn was covered with a canvas hood draped over four sheep hurdles.

Inspector Carter would have been pleased with his morning's work except that it was beginning to drizzle, and it was Saturday, and he was now nothing more than a glorified caretaker. When Major Phillips arrived in a Humber staff car with driver, Carter was relieved to be requested to join Phillips inside the house.

He confirmed that the girl and three of the men in the photographs were the people he had interviewed at the farmhouse. He also identified Schultz's photograph as being a reasonable likeness of the corpse. The damage from the death bullet was mainly at the back of Schultz's head, the hole at the front was through the left eye-socket. The sixth man, Rudi Kruger, he couldn't identify. He hadn't seen him on his previous visit and he had not seen the man who was now a corpse. Unfortunately nobody had noted the car's number but he could confirm that it was a dark-red Standard 10.

The police-station at Cranbrook had no office available of

a suitable size to house Major Phillips and his signals and admin staff, so they were to be accommodated in a building at Ashford taken over by the HQ of a platoon of the Royal Sussex Regiment. The GSO 11 (Ops) from Southern Command was on his way to join Phillips, in case troops needed to be deployed.

Seventeen

Von Bayer talked to Ushi while he was shaving. He told her what he planned and asked her if she objected. She didn't hesitate. She accepted, but insisted that Walter Kleist should not be told until they were already at the hospital. Von Bayer reluctantly agreed.

Mrs Williams, by some miracle, had produced sausages for their breakfast and after they had paid her she had waved them off as von Bayer turned the car in the drive.

Von Bayer stopped the car at the minor road that led to Ashford. They were about five miles from the town with dense woods on both sides of the road.

Von Bayer took a deep breath and turned to look at Kleist in the passenger seat beside him. Kleist's face was deathly pale, the edges of his lips were blue.

'Walter, I'm going to take you and Ushi to the hospital. You need proper treatment. And I'm going to leave you both there so that there will be no complications. You just give yourselves up. Answer any questions that you are asked, and forget all about us. You've been fantastic on this whole damn trip. Another month or two and you'll be well enough to welcome the Wehrmacht when they come over.'

Von Bayer hated every word he said. The banality, the hypocrisy, and its total inadequacy. But he could find no other words to comfort either Kleist or himself.

Kleist turned his head slowly and painfully to look at von Bayer, the big brown eyes dull with pain.

'Not ... my ... Ushi, Max ...' he sighed heavily. 'Just me.'

The silence seemed more silent because of Ushi's sobs and von Bayer's voice broke as he started to speak.

'She wants to be with you, Walter. And she's right. You're in pain.'

Kleist looked away towards the wood. Then he said softly. 'Let me think ... alone ... a few minutes. I'll walk a little.'

'You're not strong enough, Walter,' Ushi cried out.

He turned to look at her. 'I am, my love. I must.'

And his hand moved to the door-catch and the door swung open. Slowly he got out and stood up with his hands on the car roof as he steadied himself and breathed deeply.

Then he turned and walked slowly along the bridle-path to the edge of the woods. He stumbled over the roots of a tree and then he was lost in the trees. A brightly-coloured cock-pheasant followed him as if it were tame. Then, as if it knew, it took flight a second before they heard the shot.

Voss had put his arms round Ushi as von Bayer leapt out of the car. 'Don't go, Ushi. He wouldn't want you to.'

Voss held her gently as she shivered violently, as if she had an ague. She beat her forehead against his shoulder as he tried to stroke her head. Rudi Kruger's eyes were closed and he silently said a prayer – *'Vater unser, der Du bist in Himmel ...'* It was the only part of the Lord's Prayer he could remember; and he said it over and over again.

Walter Kleist was sitting with his back against the trunk of a beech tree and the blood from the back of his head stained the green lichen on the tree's grey bark. His head was on his knees where he had fallen forward, and the barrel of the pistol was still in his mouth.

Von Bayer straightened up and then walked back towards the car. When Rudi Kruger looked towards him from the car he signalled him to come.

They carried Kleist's body away from the bridle-path and covered it with bracken. There was nothing more they could do.

As they walked back together von Bayer stopped and looked at Kruger.

'What do we do, Rudi? Do we give ourselves up?'

'We do whatever you say, Herr Sturmbannführer.'

Von Bayer turned towards the car and they walked on. In the car he saw Ushi Lange still with her head on Voss's shoulder. He looked on the map. It seemed a long, long way to the deserted house at Stone-cum-Ebony. But once they were there maybe they could steal a boat from Rye or Hastings.

He started the car and headed for Great Chart.

After they were through Great Chart von Bayer turned off the main road again. They drove slowly through the lanes past the great woods of beech and oak, past the straggling cottages that signalled the approach to Shadoxhurst and Woodchurch, and then the danger point of Appledore village where, whichever road they chose to enter the village, they must inevitably get past the junction that led to Stone and the deserted farmhouse.

Von Bayer chose the road that led down the village high street, and it looked as if he were right so far. At the junction just beyond the Red Lion there was no road-block or checkpoint. He turned right and the road to Stone was clear. Up the small hill and – they were on the way down – he saw the Utility van and the two soldiers talking. There were two more further down the road. Then they were almost on top of the pole across the road. To his horror von Bayer heard the rear door open and he shouted, 'Get back in the car,' as he saw Kruger jump out, Tommy-gun in hand. And because it was Kruger he had had to shout in German. There was no way the soldiers would not have heard.

Then like some nightmare in slow motion he saw the nearest soldier fall, his gun clattering on the road and then Kruger stopped in his run, his body turned, buffeted by the bullets that sliced across him. Von Bayer let in the clutch and accelerated. For a moment the pole was dragged along clattering by the car, and then it rolled free.

He saw the Bren gun swing on its axis and felt the impact of the blow at his shoulder. Then bullets smashed across the car door and there was the pain of burning on his stomach. But they were past now and Voss shouted, 'The Bren's on a

172

fixed traverse, keep going, Max.' A rifle bullet whined off the roof of the car and then they had turned left to Stone and the hedges gave them protection.

They swung over the hump-backed bridge at the Ferry Inn and on to the junction. Sharp right at the small green, and they were in the winding narrow lane to the farmhouse. In the distance he could see the oast that marked the entrance to the driveway. Minutes later he drove the car up the slope of the drive, the cinders flying from the spinning wheels. Then at the end of the track the car bounced over the rough grass and he stopped when the farmhouse hid the car from the road.

There was warm wetness between his legs, and as he pulled aside his coat he saw that the warmth and the wetness was blood from his stomach.

He sat there without the will to move and said to Voss, 'Check out the farmhouse, Erich. We want the best field of fire, back and front.'

He watched Voss stumble across the heaps of bricks that had been the rear wall of the farmhouse. The slate roof sagged like an animal with a broken back, and where the rear rooms had been torn away he saw the sad personal guts of the house exposed. A fireplace hung down, held by one side of its metal frame. A framed print of 'The Hay Wain' still hung askew on a bedroom wall. And the white china wash-bowl hung from the wall, like some giant flower, on the stalk of its lead pipe. The crater from the bomb was full of water, although the ground was dry, and the legs of tables and remnants of chairs stuck up from the heap of rubble with torn pieces of their fabric flapping in the fitful breeze.

He closed his eyes until Voss was shaking him awake.

'The first bedroom upstairs, Max. Good field of fire and no cover for them for nearly two hundred metres.' When von Bayer didn't answer, Voss bent down to look through the car window.

'What's the matter, Max?' Then, as he saw, he said. 'For God's sake where did they get you?'

'In the belly. And I think they must have hit my shoulder.'

173

Voss opened the rear door. 'Help me, Ushi. Help me get him upstairs.'

Ushi Lange came out of her own personal nightmare when she saw the blood on von Bayer's clothes, and slowly, step by step, they held him as he struggled up the shattered stairs to the long bedroom.

Voss found bales of straw in the ramshackle barn and carried two up to the room. They spread it on the floorboards in the corner for von Bayer to lie on. Ushi found water at a bent stand-pipe near where the kitchen had once been. A small trickle emerged when she turned on the tap. As she slid off von Bayer's coat he fainted, and he was still unconscious as she eased off his jacket. He groaned as she folded back the tattered blood-stained shirt from the wound in his shoulder. With her eyes half-closed against the ghastly sight she bound both her stockings tightly over his shoulder and under his arm, padding it with a piece of cloth from his shirt, rolled into a ball.

She soaked a towel from the car in the cold water and, without the courage to look at the wound, she held it against his belly.

They were left undisturbed that night, but by the following morning a process of elimination had led their pursuers to the farmhouse.

Voss heard the squeal of brakes, and although he couldn't see the vehicle in the grey morning light he saw the group of men. One by one they ran across the drive to take cover in the low hedge. He could hear the faint shouts as somebody gave them orders.

Then there was the crackle of a loud-hailer and a voice said, 'Put down your guns and come out with your hands up.'

Voss slightly lifted the sub-machine gun where it rested on the broken window-frame, and setting the catch to 'repeat' he gave a short burst of fire.

The shots echoed eerily over the flat marshland and an echo seemed to come back from the low hills to the north.

Even in the summer the Romney Marshes are awesome

rather than beautiful, and under the leaden winter sky the landscape was gaunt and forbidding.

Voss could see no figures now, and he guessed that they were considering alternative tactics for taking the house. Mortars would do it easily enough but he guessed that they probably wanted them alive so that they could be questioned.

As the clouds lifted slightly, Voss could see the road clearly, and across the further hedge the fields already lay under a shallow sheet of water and seagulls from the coast stood unmoving on the few dry patches. He heard the engine of another vehicle arriving and then all was silent again.

Voss was not sure why he was sitting there. Von Bayer had given him no orders and looked in no shape to give orders. Voss wondered what real soldiers did in such circumstances. He felt that before long there would be a sign. Something would happen to decide the issue one way or the other. He knew that he had no wish to die and his training and instincts as a hunter had given him the virtue of patience. He would sit there and wait, but his instinct told him that it was going to be a very long day.

Eighteen

Voss was sitting on a wooden box with the barrel of the Tommy-gun still resting on the bottom edge of the window frame. At the side of his right foot were two loaded magazines, and against the wall were four boxes still unopened. Von Bayer half-sat, half-lay on the straw. His head was back, his jacket for a pillow, and his eyes were closed. His pale face was gaunt and lined, his cheeks hollow. The blood from his shoulder seemed to have stopped flowing from under the make-shift tourniquet. Ushi Lange sat watching him, holding the soaking wet cloth against his belly.

The sky was beginning to lighten when von Bayer awoke. He turned his head slowly to look at Ushi Lange, his blue eyes were blood-shot, and his mouth was open as he breathed with a shallow uneven rhythm.

'Have they gone, Ushi?'

'Not yet, Max.'

The blue eyes looked at her face and she tried not to notice the scarlet trickle of blood that slid from the corner of his mouth when he spoke.

'Where are we, Ushi?'

'In the bombed farmhouse.'

'The bombed farmhouse?' he said slowly, as if he didn't understand. 'In England?'

'Yes,' she said. 'In England. Try and rest, Max.'

There was a tear forming at the corner of his eye and as it grew it slid down to mingle with the blood at his mouth.

'Will she come, Ushi?'

'Who, Max?'

'Sadie. I want to see Sadie. Just for a few minutes.'

Ushi Lange struggled to her feet and walked across to stand next to Voss. She bent down to whisper in his ear.

'He wants to see the girl, Erich.'

'How long will he last?'

'I can't tell. I just don't know enough. A day perhaps. Even two.'

'There's no way we could contact her.'

'There *is*, Erich.'

'Tell me.'

'I could walk down to the soldiers with my arms up. They could contact the girl.'

'Why the hell should they?'

'We give ourselves up in exchange.'

'It's only a matter of time before they come for us and that'll be the end for all of us.'

'They would lose at least one when they did.'

'They're going to lose more than one.'

'So maybe they'll agree.'

He shrugged. 'Whatever you want, my dear. You're taking a risk. If you want to go, rip up a bit of white cloth and hold it up.'

'D'you mind being a prisoner, Erich?'

'All I want, Ushi, is to go to sleep. And I'd rather be a prisoner than a corpse. I've had enough.'

Her hand touched his shoulder. 'I'm going to try. Wish me luck.'

He nodded and shrugged. 'Good luck.' But his voice was flat and indifferent. He didn't even turn as she walked slowly back to kneel beside von Bayer.

Von Bayer lay just as she had left him and she knelt down beside him.

'Max. Can you hear me, Max?'

'Yes.'

'Where does Sadie live?'

He sighed and closed his eyes, trying to collect his thoughts. Finally he said slowly, 'St Michael's Lodge in Cambridge.'

'What is her family name?'

'Aarons. Sadie Aarons.' And the blood gushed from his mouth.

She stood up clumsily and walked to where the remains of the stairs went down to the heaps of rubbish outside the farmhouse. At the bottom of the stairs she pulled up her skirt and slid down her slip. She tore it along the seams and then pulled out one of the long laths from the plastered wall. She knotted the fabric to the lath so that it became a crude white flag of surrender. She looked up for a moment at the grey skies, and then made her way through the rubble.

At the edge of the house she stuck out the flag and then walked slowly into the open. She could see soldiers at each side of the entrance to the drive. The breeze tugged fitfully at the white flag as she walked down the cinder drive-way and when she could see the soldiers' faces one of them came forward to meet her. He was quite young, an officer. He stood barring the way, looking at her face and her dusty, stained and ragged clothes.

'Who are you?'

'My name is Ushi Lange. I want to talk to whoever is the officer of authority.'

'That's me,' said Phillips.

'I ask a wish, a favour in exchange for us to surrender.'

Phillips looked at her face and saw the sadness and the exhaustion there.

'What is it you want?'

'One of us is dying, he wants to speak to someone before he dies.'

'Which one of you is it who's dying'

'Max von Bayer.'

'Sturmbannführer von Bayer?'

He saw the incredulity and disbelief on her face and she said softly. 'How do you know?'

'Berlin told us.'

'My God. My God.' She shook her head slowly.

'Who does von Bayer want to talk to?'

'A girl. Her name is Sadie Aarons. She lives in Cambridge.'

'Is she German?'

'No. She's English. Jewish.'

'Are they related?'

'He loves her and I think maybe she loves him.'

He was silent for a few moments before he spoke again.

'How many of you are in there?'

'Myself, von Bayer and one other.'

'That must be Voss. Is he injured?'

'No.'

'What weapons has he got?'

'Two guns and ammunition.'

'What kind of guns?'

'Is it Thomas guns?'

'Thompson sub-machine-guns?'

'Yes. That's it.'

'Are you injured?'

'No.'

'Has Voss agreed to this?'

'Yes.'

'And von Bayer?'

'He is too far gone to understand. He just wants to see Sadie Aarons.'

'I'll see what we can do. What's the matter with von Bayer?'

'He was shot in the shoulder and in the stomach.'

'I'll get a doctor.'

They were alongside an army van with a square wooden housing. There were three aluminium steps at the rear and he signalled for her to go inside.

A sergeant in shirt-sleeves sat in front of a radio panel, a pair of headphones on his head. He pulled one back to listen to Phillips.

'Get a link for me to the Post Office at Tunbridge Wells. Tell them I want the telephone numbers in Cambridge of all the Aarons.'

He turned to the girl. 'Is that all the address you have?'

'It's St Michael's Lodge, Cambridge.'

'You've got that, Sergeant?'

'Yes, sir. I'll get cracking.'

'After that get the MO down here straightaway from Ashford.'

'Yes, sir.'

Phillips took Ushi Lange's arm and helped her back down on to the road.

'D'you want to go back or stay here?'

'I'll go back.'

'Right. Take your white flag back with you, hang it out of the window to show that Voss will not fire on our men. And wait. It may take some time. The girl may not be available and in any case Cambridge is a long journey from here. I'll see if I can raise a staff car for her.'

She sighed heavily, and he said. 'You must be glad it's all over.'

She shook her head but she didn't speak. Then they were at the driveway. 'Have you got enough food?' Phillips asked.

She looked at him. 'The doctor will be enough. Can he bring drugs for pain? We shan't be able to move him or he will haemorrhage.'

'Don't worry. He'll be here soon.'

He watched her walk up the track, stoop to pick up the tattered flag and walk to the back of the farmhouse. A few minutes later he saw it draped over the window frame of the end bedroom.

Geheimrat Lemke was never sure whether he was made to go through these sickening rituals because of the legal niceties or as a demonstration of what could happen to those who offended the leaders of the Nazi party.

The basement cell was solid concrete except for the steel door. There was no furniture, no window. It was empty except for the man who stood there with his arms on his hips watching Kästner's body slowly rotating on the thin cord that went tautly from his neck to the hook on the long iron bar that stretched from wall to wall almost nine feet from the floor. Another eighteen inches and Kästner's toes would have touched the ground. But there hadn't been another eighteen inches and Kästner's face was purple as it lay awkwardly against his shoulder.

The Gestapo doctor had already pronounced Kästner dead but the subject had to have been dead for fifteen minutes before the man was allowed to lift down the corpse, and Geheimrat Lemke had to identify the body as that of Kästner, Otto. Former Oberst in the Abwehr.

Ludwig von Bayer was the last to get out of the railway carriage and as he stepped awkwardly and uncertainly down to the railway station platform he saw the sign that said 'Oranienburg'. He wore his winter-coat and his good leather shoes, and in his hand he held a small brown-paper bag that held his toilet and shaving things wrapped up in a small towel.

The two SS men shouted their orders, and the twenty or so men trudged off up the wet road in the rain.

Although it was only two miles to the concentration camp he was sweating and panting as they went through the wide gates. He held himself aloof from the rest of them because he was sure that when his lawyer had sorted things out this little trip would be no more than a talking-point at board-room lunches. But he was disturbed when he found that the prisoner who entered his details in the camp record-book was none other than the former Judge Meyer of the Berlin Appellate Court. And Meyer ignored his greeting as if he hadn't spoken.

The doctor came an hour later. He was an RAMC captain. Elderly, and complete with a competent-looking black bag.

Ushi went down the rickety stairway to meet him. He looked at her without curiosity. 'I hear you've got an injured man here. What's the trouble?'

'He's been shot in the shoulder and in the stomach.'

'I see. Well, take me up to see him. Can you produce any hot water?'

'I'm afraid not.'

'Cold water?'

'Yes. A little.'

The captain glanced at Voss in passing as he walked over to the corner where von Bayer lay on the straw. He stood looking at him for a moment, bag in hand. Then he put down his bag, slid off his greatcoat and knelt down in the straw.

Slowly and gently he unwound the bandage from von Bayer's shoulder. Ushi turned away as it exposed the gleaming white bone where the flesh had been torn away. He reached for his bag, opened it, and sprinkled some yellow powder from a small metal container on to a pad of cotton-wool. Very lightly he touched the open wound with the pad.

Then he carefully and gently lifted von Bayer's hand from his belly and pulled away the blood-soaked cloth. The wound was like an open mouth and he guessed it must have been a ricochet to have opened the flesh so wide. His finger and thumb moved to von Bayer's wrist and he looked at his watch. Gently placing the hand at von Bayer's side the doctor took out his stethoscope and put it over the heart. He listened for a long time and then put the stethoscope back in his bag.

He put two fingers under von Bayer's rib-cage and pressed gently. Von Bayer groaned and blood gurgled at the mouth of the wound. The doctor took out a hypodermic and loaded it from a phial. He swabbed near the inside of von Bayer's elbow, pinched up a vein, and then slid in the needle.

He stood up slowly and then bent to close his bag. As he walked towards the stairs he nodded to Ushi to follow him.

At the foot of the broken stairs he turned to face her.

'There's nothing anybody can do. If we tried to move him he would bleed to death before we got him to the ambulance. I'd guess the bullet is still inside and it's done major damage to several organs. He's bleeding internally, but it's quite slow.' He looked at her. 'Is he your man?'

'No. Just a very close friend.'

'I understand you're staying with him until some girl comes?'

'Yes.'

'You know that he's dying?'

'I wasn't sure.'

'Depending on the rate of bleeding it could be two hours or even two days. He's got a strong heart. I've given him a shot that will kill the pain. The effect will last for about four hours. I'm going to leave you the hypodermic and a dozen shots. Put the needle in roughly the same spot in the vein. By tomorrow he'll need them every two hours. Can you cope?'

'I don't understand "Cope".'

'Can you manage. Can you do what I have asked you to do?'

'Yes.'

'I'll check you over yourself when this lot is over.' He looked at her face. 'You'd better warn the girl of his condition when she comes.'

'I will.'

'Right. I'll be on my way then.'

He turned, and then hesitated, and turned to look at her again.

'You're a good girl,' he said solemnly, and then turned and walked away.

She sat beside von Bayer, sometimes sleeping, fighting to stay awake. It was almost midnight. She had given him one injection and was preparing the second when she heard footsteps on the stairs, stumbling about in the dark. Then as she turned she saw the faint light of a shielded torch. She walked quickly to the head of the stairs. She could see a man in the dim light from the torch.

He said quietly. 'Where is Max?'

'Who *are* you?'

'My name is Aarons. Moshe Aarons. Where is he?'

'I was expecting Sadie.'

'Where is Max?'

'In the corner, I'll lead the way.' She stopped, and whispered. 'He's dying. I think he's just been hanging on for Sadie.'

They passed Voss sleeping stretched out under the window on the bare boards, his hand loosely closed over the stock of the sub-machine-gun.

Aarons shone the torch on von Bayer's face and then knelt down in the straw beside him. He took von Bayer's hand in his.

'Can you hear me, Max?'

It was a long time before von Bayer spoke.

'Who is it?'

'It's Moshe Aarons, Max.'

The blue eyes slowly opened, trying to look at Aarons' face.

'Not Sadie. I wanted Sadie. Why wouldn't she come?'

And the tears poured now, silently, down von Bayer's cheeks.

'She *couldn't* come, Max.'

Von Bayer moved his head to look better at Aarons.

'Why?' he whispered. 'Tell me why.'

Aarons took a deep breath. 'She's dead, Max. She was killed in an air-raid. They bombed the Guildhall School.'

'When?'

'Ten days ago.'

Von Bayer closed his eyes and groaned.

'I loved her so much, Moshe.'

'I'm sure you did, my boy.'

'Every day I thought about her.'

'She kept all your rosettes on the wall in her room. She spoke about you often.'

'Why did *you* come, Moshe?'

'They told me you were badly hurt.'

'You must hate me.'

'Why should I do that?'

'All this. The war. Sadie. All of it.'

'You and Sadie didn't want a war, Max. Like so many others, you're just victims.'

'But I'm a German.'

'And Sadie was a Jew. And it didn't matter until the Nazis made it matter. And you wouldn't be here if it were not for the Nazis.'

Von Bayer was silent for a few moments, and then he said, 'Don't watch me die, Moshe.' He looked up to see Moshe Aarons' face in the faint light of the torch.

'Say something nice to me, Moshe, before you go.'

Aarons was silent for only a few moments as he collected his thoughts, but it seemed a long, long time before he spoke.

'Do you remember a song Sadie used to sing to us all? It was called "Loch Lomond".'

' "The bonnie, bonnie banks . . ." was that it?'

'Yes. Do you remember the lines that went – "You'll take the low road and I'll take the high road and I'll be in Scotland before you"?'

'Yes. I could never understand them.'

'Well, it was after one of the terrible battles between the Scots and the English. A Highland officer was taken prisoner and was imprisoned in one of the English border towns to be executed. They gave him a last wish, and he asked to see his girl. And that was what he sang to her at their last meeting. He said that she would take the low-road back to Scotland, and he would take the high-road – the heavenly road. And he would be in Scotland before her.' He paused and then said softly. 'And that's you and Sadie, Max.'

He bent forward, put his lips to the young man's cold forehead and said softly, 'Shalom'. Then he stood up and walked across the room to the head of the stairs.

Ushi Lange knelt down beside von Bayer taking his hand in hers.

'Will you do something for me, Ushi?'

'Of course.'

'There's a package in my jacket wrapped in yellow oilskins. Will you bury it in the earth, here in this house?'

'Of course.'

He sighed. 'Kiss me goodbye, Ushi.'

She kissed his bloody mouth, and stayed with him until he died, half an hour later.

On 5 July 1943 a Vosper patrol boat had left Dover Harbour and headed to a rendezvous just clear of the Goodwin Sands, where a German E-boat was already waiting. Ushi Lange had been tried, *in camera*, and sentenced to seven years' imprisonment. She stepped from the Royal Navy patrol boat to the E-boat and turned to watch the captured SOE radio operator make her way on to the British boat. There were salutes on both sides, and then the two boats backed off and headed for their home ports. And that night there was an empty cell in Holloway Jail for women, and an empty cell in

Fresnes prison in Paris where the Gestapo incarcerated its captured enemy agents of the SOE.

When Germany was occupied Ushi Lange became an interpreter for the Military Government detachment that covered Regierungsbezirk Hanover. A few years later she married a captain in the US Army who was an announcer on the American Forces Network. They now live in Los Angeles where he works for KJOI, a sweet-music radio station she enjoys. They have two girls and it wasn't until the eldest was five years old that her husband had ever heard her sing.

Erich Voss served ten years of his fifteen-year sentence and died in Nairobi three years after he was released. His small pyrethrum farm was quite successful and is now owned by the Kenya Government.

Max von Bayer's body was buried, at the Aarons family's request, in the churchyard of the Garrison Church in Cambridge. It's roughly ten minutes' walk from there to the cemetery where a stone remembers Sadie Aarons, whose body, if it *was* recovered from the rubble of the Guildhall School of Music, was never identified as hers.

Rudi Kruger's body lies in a churchyard in Ashford. His wife never learned why he didn't come back from the SS motor school. Maybe it was considered a security risk, or maybe it was just Nazi spite. In the end it didn't matter. She was raped and killed by the first Russian patrol that swept through the workers' estate in Wedding at the fall of Berlin.

Nobody has ever traced Ludwig von Bayer. He was never released from the concentration camp, and, with thousands of emaciated corpses unidentified, it was assumed that his must have been one of them.